The First Life of Andy McCurdy

A Novel By

Eben Dobson

This is a work of fiction. Names, characters, places and incidents are either a product of the author's imagination or are used fictitiously, and any resemblance to actual persons, living or dead, business establishments, events, or locales is entirely coincidental.

"The First Life of Andy McCurdy," by Eben Dobson. ISBN 1-58939-787-8 (softcover); 1-58939-805-x (hardcover).

Published 2005 by Virtualbookworm.com Publishing Inc., P.O. Box 9949, College Station, TX 77842, US. ©2005, Eben Dobson. All rights reserved. No part of this publication may be reproduced, stored in a retrieval system, or transmitted in any form or by any means, electronic, mechanical, recording or otherwise, without the prior written permission of Eben Dobson.

Manufactured in the United States of America.

DEDICATION

To my wife, Sonia, for helping me at every turn and for putting up with the inordinate amount of time I took to write this short book.

Acknowledgements

Lynn Marx for her tireless proofreading.

Fred Hay for his imaginative art.

Alexis Garrett for her helpful criticisms.

Some members of my family and a few friends for reading early versions and encouraging me.

Early March - 1970

The Vietnam War was a quagmire, and college campuses were ablaze with riots. Thousands were dying in the war while four hundred thousand gathered in the rain at Woodstock to listen to Joan Baez, Jimi Hendrix, the Grateful Dead and a host of others. A deep chasm had split the adult establishment from the rebellious youth.

It was during this time that Andy McCurdy told of his death-defying adventure aboard a fifty-foot sailboat in Mexico.

Andy described himself as lacking self-confidence and incurably irresponsible, with no ambition in his life beyond sharing a joint on the beach with the girl of his dreams – his stepsister. His appearance, like that of his entire generation, was dogged and unoriginal. But what set him apart was his preference to do things with his parents. This was the basis for the maturity of his thoughts and his ability to express them.

He saw himself as useless and at the top of God's shit list, but as hair-raising events exposed him to death, his courage and resourcefulness prevailed.

Prologue

Thousands of years ago, a portion of the east wall of Todos Santos, a volcanic island, eroded away to the sea, forming a boat anchorage snug in all weather (except a southeast blow). Only sixty miles south of San Diego and eight miles out of Ensenada, Todos Santos was an easily-reached paradise for cruising sailors. The little island's hills and valleys were matted with wild flowers in the spring and with green succulents and a heather-like plant the rest of the year. The harbor provided a sanctuary for gulls and pelicans, and an underwater haven for sea anemones, garibaldi, seals and thousands of other types of sea life.

Tom and Rosa Bryce knew the island intimately for they had sailed their forty-foot sloop, the Wind Song, there countless times. But this time, the circumstances were different.

The couple had just completed an eight-day beat to windward from Cabo San Lucas, the southern tip of Baja California. The wind and the sea had relentlessly stormed out of the northwest, pounding and pitching the boat head-on, making motor-sailing tediously slow and fatiguing.

Normally, they would not have sailed this way. They knew the trip could be a miserable, uphill battle, so they would have picked and chosen their runs, taking advantage of the comfortable protection offered by Magdalena and Turtle Bay and Cedros and San Martin Island.

But this time, they were not making the decisions.

It had been a gloriously starry evening, and the Bryces had been enjoying a rum and tonic after finishing preparations for an early morning departure. The serenity of the evening had been interrupted by a couple in a rubber dinghy rowing alongside the Wind Song. The man had rowed while a woman sat straddle-legged over the bow, her bare feet trailing in the water. She had called the Bryces by name and said they had mutual friends in San Diego. The couple was invited aboard, and seconds later the woman had jammed a .38-caliber pistol into Rosa's stomach. The man grabbed Tom from behind and held a long-bladed knife to his throat.

The short and stocky female intruder had straight red hair with bangs, and had done most of the talking. She had ordered Tom and Rosa below deck, using her pistol as a prodder. The man, who had kinky yellow hair and a long nose that had surely been broken more than once, had taken two jerry jugs of gasoline from his Avon and stowed them on the foredeck, lashing them to the mast. He had also brought aboard an outboard engine. Quickly he partially deflated the Avon dinghy and stowed it over the sailboat's cabin top. By the time he had swung down the companionway into the main cabin, his partner had already forced Tom and Rosa onto their backs, hands behind their heads. The woman had jammed her pistol barrel into Rosa's mouth, chipping a front tooth and slightly cutting her lower lip, emphasizing that if they wanted to stay alive, specific behavior would be required until they reached their northern destination.

The First Life of Andy McCurdy

Thirty minutes before dawn, Tom was at the helm moving the Wind Song slowly forward as Rosa, from the bow, operated the electric windlass to take up the anchor. Through the companionway, from below deck, the broken-nosed man named Bruno and his girlfriend, Angel, kept the kidnapped couple under close surveillance. The kidnappers instructed Tom to steer clear of all other boats and head directly for the rocks at the tip of Cabo San Lucas, then swing northwest into the Pacific until land was out of sight. If anyone waved a good-bye, Tom and Rosa were to return the gesture with their usual enthusiasm.

As they headed for the cape, Tom could just see John Swingler waving a farewell salute from his beautiful ninety-foot ketch, the Lobo del Mar. Tom waved back as instructed. It would be the last time in his life that Tom would see a friend.

After eight days and one two-hour stop for diesel fuel in Turtle Bay, the Wind Song anchored in the cove of Todos Santos Island. Tom was ordered to phone his son in La Jolla via the KOU San Diego marine operator. He was to say that they were resting up in Todos Santos and would be leaving before sunrise; so expect them home the next afternoon.

After the radio call, the Bryces were told that they would be set free on the island. The probability of this happening was not calculated by Tom or Rosa. Days and nights of fear had rendered them incapable of orderly thought processes. Fatigued and pressed to the outer limits of sanity, any hope concerning their survival was accepted without reservation.

To ensure that Tom used a normal voice tone and gave no other signals to alert officials to their situation, Angel ordered Rosa to lie on the starboard bunk. Again, she jammed a pistol barrel into Rosa's mouth. One of Rosa's eyes was swollen shut from a previous beating; her other eye stared frantically at the ceiling as she fought not to gag.

Tom, ashen and gaunt from sleeplessness, mustered every ounce of poise he had left to create a normal voice. He knew that what hope they had for life rested on his ability to stay calm and perform as he had been ordered. With the help of usual VHF static, the radio call ended without any apparent suspicion.

"Wind Song – this is San Diego marine operator – do you have any more traffic?"

"No operator," answered Tom. "This is the Wind Song – Whiskey Zulu Nectar 1791 clear with your station."

Bruno swiped the radio switch off with his left hand then, with his right hand, slashed at Tom's throat with his long-bladed knife, severing both carotid arteries. Simultaneously, Angel pulled the trigger of her revolver, firing a bullet through the roof of Rosa's mouth that blasted into her brain.

The Avon had already been inflated and placed in the water with care to not damage the one million dollars of powder cocaine that had been inserted inside her inflatable sides. Bruno placed the jerry jugs of gasoline in the dinghy and remounted the outboard engine.

The Wind Song powered out of Todos Santos Cove for the last time. She headed north, then three miles beyond the island she stopped dead in the water. All the electrical switches were turned off and the valves for the butane stove and oven were fully opened. After tightly shutting the hatch, Tom and Rosa's murderers climbed into their Avon. Two pulls and their outboard started and they were speeding for San Diego at thirty miles per hour. The northwest wind had totally abated, rendering a flat

The First Life of Andy McCurdy

calm sea – perfect conditions for traveling.

Fifteen minutes had passed before a time-fuse fired a spark on the cabin floor of the Wind Song. Instantly, the butane-filled boat exploded and an inferno of flame burst up and beyond her forty-five-foot mast.

Two hours later, the rubber dinghy passed Point Loma Light and entered San Diego Harbor. Bruno had already sunk the jerry jugs into deep water, and as they neared Kona Kai Point, he stopped the outboard, unlocked it from the transom and let it sink into forty feet of water.

The couple casually rowed past the harbor police dock, past the Kona Kai anchorage and directly to E dock of the San Diego Yacht Club. Bruno carefully deflated the Avon on the dock while Angel retrieved a large push-cart. In minutes they were exiting on a ramp that ran directly by a very active clubhouse bar. The participants of a T.G.I.F. party had thanked God enough times to be mellow and oblivious to the unfamiliar couple walking past them. It would not be until the next day that the partygoers would learn that at about the time they had ordered their first round of cocktails, two popular members of their club had been murdered and were now little more than ash in the ocean waters near Ensenada, Mexico.

So far Bruno and Angel's plan of action was running perfectly. The most blatant retreat was the least obvious. During early evening, messing around with dinghies and sabots was a common practice, especially on Friday nights. So, although the plan was insidious, the San Diego Yacht Club provided the perfect location for the killers to exit their crime.

In the northwest corner of the yacht club parking lot, Bruno and Angel loaded the deflated dinghy into the trunk of a model 164E Volvo. The car had a yacht club sticker on its left front window and, as they drove through the club's main gate, the guard gave a cheery salute. One minute later, they turned off Shelter Island Drive and stopped near Kettenburg Boat Yard. Angel got out of the car and ripped the yacht club sticker off the windshield then got back in.

In another eight minutes, as they pulled to the curb in front of the San Diego Airport, an immaculately dressed man in a blue suit stepped behind the Volvo. His name was Leonard Peters. Bruno got out, popped the trunk and, with his pocket knife, slit open a section of the rubber dinghy. Several small packets were revealed. Peters made a careful inspection, then nodded approvingly.

Next he pointed to a small overnight bag and said, "Your fee and two tickets. You've got twenty minutes to catch the last Pacific Southwest Airlines flight to San Francisco."

"How do we know the money is all there," whined Bruno.

"It's all there because I say it's all there. But, Bruno, if it's not all there, there's nothing you can do about it," said Peters with a smirk.

By the time the pair was airborne, Leonard Peters had driven the Volvo to Interstate 5, heading north for Los Angeles. Miles away, the forgotten Wind Song, with her hull burnt to the waterline and her contents incinerated, cast a red glow on the water as she slowly drifted toward the north beach of Punta Banda, where Mexican fishermen would discover her before sunrise.

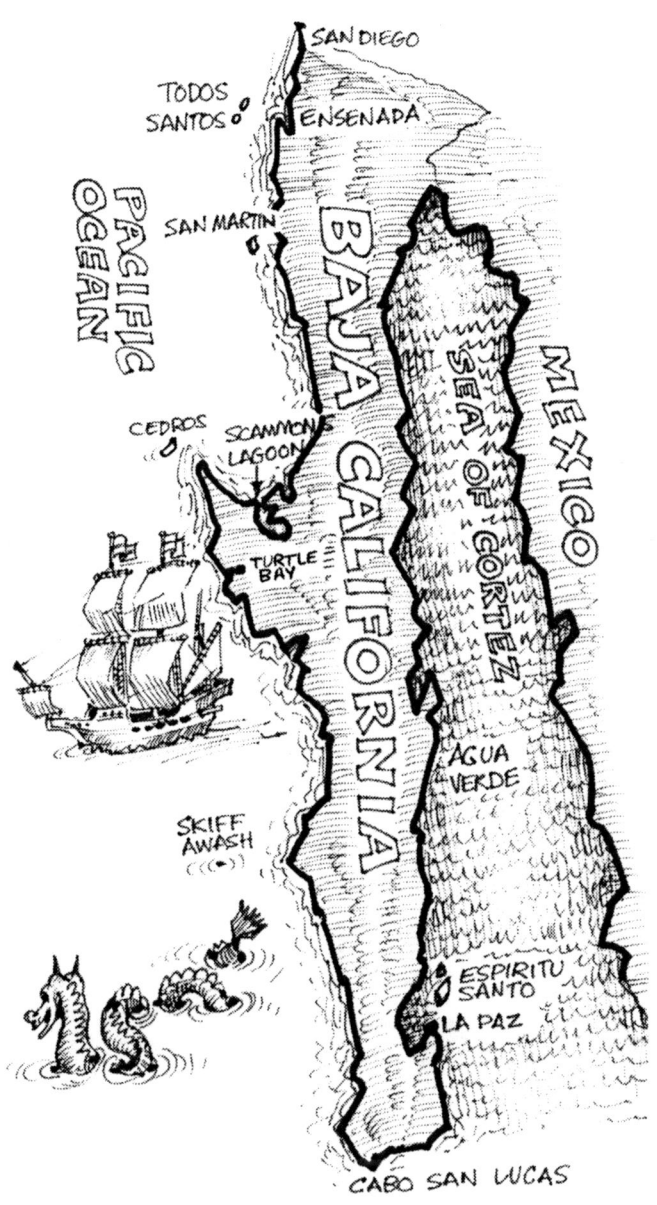

Chapter One

The evening was quiet and the sky was a blanket of stars. I stretched out my sleeping bag in the open cockpit of our 50-foot Kettenburg, the Sumac. In seconds my sleepy eyes were tracking a curve from the handle of the Big Dipper to find Arcturus, a magnificent first-dimensional star. It seemed like only a few minutes had passed when a noise on the dock startled me awake. A man was deflating a dinghy so I got up and offered my assistance, but he made it quite obvious that he considered my gesture to be an intrusion. I assumed that he was professional crew from a visiting boat. He was too salty to be a member of the yacht club, and even in the dark the distortion of his face was quite noticeable. A bent-to-one-side nose was the centerpiece of a face that must have been smashed with a coal shovel more than once. His red-headed girlfriend was equally unfriendly and almost as ugly; so it was no disappointment that they departed quickly, allowing me to recapture the tranquility of the night.

When I awoke, the morning sun was already drying the dew that glistened on the deck of the Sumac. It had taken me hours to fall back asleep. The anticipation of our voyage was part of it, but for some reason the weird couple with the dinghy haunted me. Besides their unfriendliness, there was something else about them that felt out of place.

'Enough about that,' I thought, 'this is the day of our departure and there are more exciting things to think about!' The sounds of the bay and the warmth of the morning held me in a dreamy state. With my eyes closed, I listened to the seagulls scolding each other and the halyards gently slapping against masts and all the rest that made the morning music of a harbor.

My morning reverie would soon end, for my father, (actually, my stepfather), would be arriving and final preparations for our afternoon departure would be underway.

My stepfather's name is Elliot McCurdy, but hardly anyone knows his first name. Everyone, even his kids, calls him Mac. Nothing else sounds right.

My real father's name was Andrew Finney, (that's my name, too), and he was killed in Korea. He and Mac were in a fighter squadron together at K2, an air base near Taegue, Korea. They flew several tough missions against a North Korean bridge complex called Sinanju. Apparently, the bridges spanned a deep mountain gorge and were heavily fortified with anti-aircraft guns. My dad was on a low-level bombing run when his F-84 took a direct hit. He never pulled out of his dive. Mac was flying on his wing and saw him go in.

After the war, Mac went home to discover that his wife had found better things to do than wait around and wonder if she would become a widow of a fighter pilot. Instead, she went off with some sort of an evangelistic preacher, leaving Mac with full custody of their two-year-old daughter.

Thank God for that, for she became my stepsister and I'm crazy about her. I'll explain that in a bit.

The First Life of Andy McCurdy

Anyway, not long after Mac's wife ran out on him, he went to see my mom. I guess they commiserated about their misfortunes, fell in love, married, and my last name got changed to McCurdy.

Because my real dad died before I was born, I never physically knew him. But I really do know him, and get to know him better everyday through the wonderful stories Mac and Mom tell me.

Considering the times, my relationship with my parents was abnormal. I liked doing things with them – especially sailing. So, obviously, I am just not in the groove with my generation. I look just as ratty as they do with my long hair, dirty jeans and bare feet, but I am different inside. I like to read a lot, and my mom claims that my vocabulary is probably bigger than hers and definitely bigger than Mac's. That also sets me apart, for my friends don't seem to know any adjectives other than "bitchen."

My generation burns a lot of energy hating the establishment – mainly because of the Vietnam War. When my pals heard that my joy in life was cruising on a sailboat with my parents, they wanted to puke. That didn't bother me. I guess we are all avoiding the real world, just in different ways.

Now let's see, Mom and Mac have been married about fourteen years. I am sixteen and my stepsister is a year older than me. I imagine that you already get the drift that when I say that I am crazy about Maggie, it explains a lot about me. Given the choice of all the girls in the world, (well, not quite), but I picked my stepsister! I want to touch her all the time, and the feelings are pretty much mutual. I know it's obvious to our parents and its driving them nuts.

I'm not sure when their suspicions were confirmed, but a few months ago one particular incident certainly caught their attention. They had ducked out of a boring dinner party and caught Maggie and me in the shower together. No, we weren't in the act. We hadn't gone that far, mainly because I had some hang-ups. I just felt that Maggie was special and I didn't want to do anything that might hurt her or cause any regrets. Besides, Mac is my hero and betraying his trust would ride on my conscience forever. This wouldn't faze most kids. They think parents are for the birds. They relegate them into one big category: the establishment, a clueless mass that completely misses out on the essentials of life, like peace and love.

Leaving it at that wouldn't be completely honest. Besides hurting Maggie and betraying Mac, there was another reason. The fact is that I was just not that sure of myself. I had a bagful of insecurities that kept nagging because I didn't know how to deal with them. You'll soon see what I mean.

Well, it doesn't take a genius to sense some long-range parental planning. Mac and Mom sent Maggie off to the University of Oregon and I was aimed at a two-month Baja sailing adventure. Actually, Maggie and I had agreed with them; we were way too young and inexperienced to spin a cocoon around ourselves. Our nightly walks down Sea Lane to our favorite North La Jolla beach were magnificent, but we both recognized that the real world was out there and we both had a lot to learn.

So did Joey, that impish little brother of mine, but let me start with Annie because she came first. In fact, she proudly claims to be a honeymoon baby, born nine months to the day after Mac and Mom's wedding. A bit over a year later, my parents produced Joey. I refer to him as an imp, because that's what he is. He's way too smart for his age, and catches on to everything, including beating me

The First Life of Andy McCurdy

at backgammon and chess. He's also a constant threat to any covert activity between Maggie and me.

"Rise and shine, daylight in the swamps, hit the deck, Andy," shouted Mac before his feet hit the dock.

Doc Brush and Lizzie Walker accompanied him, so the gang, except for Mom, was all there and our trip to Baja would be underway before sunset! Doc and Mac had been pals forever. They both grew up in Minnesota and eventually moved to California. In the late fifties, Mac sold his small Minneapolis insurance agency and started a new one in La Jolla. About the same time, Doc moved his veterinary practice from Long Lake, a little town west of Minneapolis, to Del Mar and started to devote much of his time to marine biology. He's a loner, never married, and a frequent guest at our dinner table. Sometimes, when the candles are burning low (and Doc and Mac have had a little extra red wine), they tell legendary stories. My favorite is the one about Mac's old cat, Tiger.

Mac and Doc claim that Tiger had somehow been shut in the deep freezer and wasn't found for several hours. As a perfunctory gesture, and even though it was late in the evening, Mac had rushed him over to Doc's office. Tiger was still hard as a rock when he got there. Mac said the cat sort of went 'clunk' when he sat him down on the stainless-steel examining table, but Doc knew just what to do. He took an eyedropper and squirted a substance down old Tiger's throat. Sometimes they said it was brandy, sometimes gasoline, but more than often, they said it was 'obble gobble juice,' a potent, secret substance created by Doc. There are those that think the only throats this substance went down that night were Doc's and Mac's, and Tiger just thawed out on his own.

I already said that Doc didn't have a wife, but Lizzie Walker is his girlfriend and they have been together ever since Doc moved to Del Mar. Well, maybe not completely together, because they each have their own cottages in the hills above Del Mar. Lizzie is a really easy-going person close to Mom's age. She tells great jokes, and all the men love her because she is warm and friendly and because she has big boobs. Her dad was a career Marine, and all those years growing up on a Marine base taught Lizzie some wicked language. It takes about one drink for her to cut loose. Doc is normally her target.

"Jesus Christ, Doc, you are a dumb asshole," Lizzie will say, and Doc will calmly reply, "Sweet talk will get you nowhere, my dear."

Lizzie had a husband who died a long time ago, leaving her with two boys who are now teenagers. Although Doc is quite tolerant, I believe he agrees with Mac who says that they are both a brick short of a load. Hardly a week goes by when one of them doesn't try to see how many of his bones he can break. Not long ago, the youngest one went to sleep on the toilet. He slipped off the pot and cracked his head open on the bathtub. No bones were broken, but it did take thirty-one stitches to get his scalp back on right. At any rate, my guess is that those two boys are the main reason that Doc and Lizzie keep separate quarters.

In shorter time than it took me to give you that background, Mac, Doc and Lizzie arrived on the

Sumac and were waiting in the cockpit for me to bring up some coffee. Then a strange thing happened. The yacht club's flag was raised, but when it reached the top, the attendant slowly lowered it back down to half-mast.

Doc noticed it first, saying, "Looks like another member must have croaked."

"Yeah, wonder who," said Mac. At about the same second, Ron, the club manager, stepped out on the main club deck above us.

"What's the story with the flag at half-mast," shouted Doc.

"Awful news, give me a minute and I'll come down and share it with you," answered Ron.

Just as I brought the coffee up, Ron arrived and said, "You know the Bryces, owners of the Wind Song, just down a few slips from you? Well, a San Diego Coast Guard cutter just reported the discovery of their sloop, burnt to the water line. No survivors. Probable cause was a butane explosion."

"Oh my God, I can't believe it," moaned Doc. "Tom Bryce was so careful and detail-minded. Why, he wouldn't think of shutting down for the night without turning all the butane valves off, even at the outside tank."

"They weren't anchored for the night. They had been in the cove at Todos Santos but they left in the evening. The hull was found on the beach, a few miles north of the island... The Bryces were undoubtedly killed instantly," said Ron.

"How do you know they stopped at Todos Santos," I heard myself ask. My voice felt as if it came from inside a tunnel, and my mind was consumed with the image of a boat filled with butane. A spark, and then instant death. Or was there a moment to think, a moment of living horror? Or were the Bryces simply part of the simultaneous explosion and fire, the disintegration of material and the suffocation of life?

"They had radioed their son in San Diego last

night to say that they were snug at anchor in the cove," said Ron. "Probably rest–"

But before he could finish, Doc interrupted, "Well, why the hell would they go out to sea in the middle of the night?"

"Maybe they couldn't sleep. Even better, the sea was a flat calm, so why not move on?" reasoned Mac.

"No, that's just the way you would do it, 'cause you're a night-cruising fool," said Doc.

"Well, what's your theory, Doc? Pirates or something?" quipped Mac.

"Well, maybe," said Doc in a less than convincing tone. "Happened to a cruising couple out of Newport a couple of years ago. They were heading back from Baja and fell off the map. Never found a sign of the people, but their boat showed up about a year later in Hawaii – all cleaned up and painted a different color."

"So there's probably a nasty little band of Mexicans that come storming out from shore at night and pounce on rich American yachtsmen, steal all their stuff, and then blow the shit out of their boats," said Mac sarcastically.

"Yeah, maybe, except it doesn't have to be Mexicans," said Doc as he burped.

It wasn't really a burp, more like a giant hiccup. He does that a lot, particularly after brief arguments with Mac. They argue over just about everything, but never seriously. Mac always wins because conceding is against his nature, regardless of the weakness of his position. Anyway, Doc really didn't care that much, and besides, prolonged arguing aggravated his hiatal hernia, which gave him heartburn, which made him burp and increased his already enormous consumption of Arm & Hammer.

"Well, I guess we can sit here and commiserate over the fate of the Wind Song forever, but it won't do them or us much good," said Doc.

"And besides, we'll know more after the Coast Guard's done investigating," added Ron.

Chapter Two

The news of the Wind Song tragedy spread quickly around the docks of the San Diego Yacht Club, dampening the excitement of our Baja departure.

"Maybe we should delay our trip a few days," mused Lizzie.

"What the hell good is that going to do?" answered Doc.

Doc and Lizzie were set to leave by noon on their forty-foot Sea Wolf ketch. Doc was anxious; he had been commissioned by Scripps Oceanography to do a study on the gray whales while their winter migration was on.

I was relieved to hear Mac say that he agreed with Doc. We would be leaving an hour before sunset, just as planned. So after a couple more Doc burps and under a subdued atmosphere, we all turned our attention to making our final preparations. Doc and Lizzie had their boat ready to go, except for some last minute stuff, like packing in one hundred pounds of ice, topping off their water tanks, and Lizzie's final store run for two more bottles of rum.

"One thing is for sure, we won't be running out of rum. Maybe we'll run short of food and water, but not rum," said Doc with a snicker.

Just before their departure, Doc huddled with Mac. I wasn't included in the conversation but I guessed it was about the Bryce's fate. In my opinion, neither Doc nor Mac subscribed to the accident theory. There was little doubt in my mind that they intended to delve into the very heart of the mystery.

Two compelling facts were sure to fan the flames of their curiosity. The first was that Tom and Rosa Bryce were their friends, and we were all bound by the fraternal commitment of cruising sailors. The second was that Mac and Doc had identically compelling natures; they both leaped, without reservation, at the opportunity to become embroiled in anything resembling a mystery.

After some first-for-the-day smiles and some warm goodbyes, Lizzie pulled in the bow lines as Doc backed the Sirius, (named after the brightest star in the sky), out of her slip and pointed her bow toward the main channel.

"Call us tonight after you drop anchor in Todos Santos," yelled Mac. "We'll be monitoring Channel Sixteen."

Our plan was to sail through to the island of San Martin, 165 miles south of San Diego. We would be passing on the outside of Todos Santos during the night. Doc and Lizzie were stopping, though, because Doc was interested in sea anemones, and no place provided finer specimens than Todos Santos. In a day or two they would move on to Scammon's Lagoon, which was the major winter home of the gray whales. I had heard Doc say that these whales travel over six thousand miles from the Bering Sea to breed and do their calving in the lagoon. Part of Doc's plan was to attempt an actual count to help ascertain the whale's numbers after almost being massacred out of existence. In fact, twice since Charles Scammon discovered the lagoon about one hundred and fifty years ago, the gray whales had come close to extinction. But since 1937 they had been protected. Doc expected to find close to four hundred.

Around mid-afternoon, Mom and my little brother and sister showed up, and we all got into doing final chores to ready the Sumac for the long voyage.

Incidentally, Joey gets credit for the Sumac's name. Shortly after we bought her, she was in the boat yard getting her bottom painted. Her beautiful hourglass-shaped hull and her varnished mahogany cabin trunk made her look remarkably graceful. We were all awe-struck and simultaneously started spouting out names. There were lots of contenders, but Joey, out of the blue, hit the nail on the head.

"Let's call her Sumac. Don't you guys get it, 'Sue-Mac'?" (I guess I forgot to tell you that my mom's name is Susan.) We all looked at each other approvingly as Joey did a dumb little victory dance around the Sumac's keel. That same afternoon, in big, dark blue letters, SUMAC was painted on her transom. The next evening, along the dock directly in front of the San Diego Yacht Club, she was officially christened as Mom broke a bottle of champagne on the CQR anchor that stuck out from the Sumac's bow.

Before long the christening party onboard the Sumac had boiled down to the usuals, Doc, Lizzie and us. To no one's surprise, as the obble gobbles started flowing, so did the stories. The one about testing our new dinghy was a favorite.

When we bought the Sumac, she came with an eight-foot fiberglass dinghy that was carried on stern davits, so a more seaworthy rubber dinghy was on our shopping list. The field was quickly narrowed down to either the Zodiac or the Avon. The eight-foot Zodiac won on no more merit than her salesman doing a better job.

Minutes after we got our newest family toy home, Mac disclosed a testing plan. Immediately after lunch, Maggie, Joey, Annie and I were to lug the dinghy over to our neighbor's pool. We didn't have a pool because, living only a block from the ocean, Mac felt it was an unnecessary luxury.

"Besides," he would say, "why even consider a pool when your neighbor has a perfectly adequate one?"

Mom asked him once if he felt the same way about wives, but I don't recall her getting any response.

As we prepared for the inaugural launch, Mac surprised us with a secret purchase: a brand-new, three-horse Seagull outboard. (If you don't know about outboard engines, the British-made Seagull is the best.)

I was elected to pump up the Zodiac. The salesman had boasted that it would be a three-minute job, so when I was about halfway done, Mom said skeptically, "Your three minutes are up."

In another couple of minutes I had the dinghy as hard as a rock, so we strapped on the Seagull and *presto* it started with the first pull! Unfortunately, our planning had not gone much beyond that point. Our spellbound group was totally amazed at the brief time it took the little dinghy to eat up the forty-foot long swimming pool. Luckily, the pool was quite full so the voyage ended suddenly but without disaster, as we beached ourselves on the pool patio.

Normally, such a fiasco would sponsor a "Let's call it a day," but not when Mac's involved. He announced phase two before the dinghy had stopped its ridiculous skid across the concrete.

"Obviously we need a real body of water to finish our testing, so I'm proposing we move to Oceanside Harbor. Any volunteers?"

Mom refused instantly, saying, "Enough is enough, the whole thing is crazy. What more is there to learn about a stupid rubber dinghy?"

Maggie bowed out a little more graciously by saying, "I'd love to, but I have another commitment."

As usual, I was left with my mouth hanging open and nothing coming out, so I started to deflate the dinghy in preparation for the drive to Oceanside. Annie and Joey, being too young to know to object, tagged along, and soon we had the Seagull in place again on the stern of the Zodiac.

"Looks like the inlet might be building up a nasty surf break with the wind out of the south," said Mac.

"Yep, certainly should be a more solid test than Ruth's pool," I muttered faintly.

Getting through the surf line at the harbor entrance was no problem. We waited for a lull and then skimmed over a couple of small rollers before bouncing almost straight up when we hit a breaker head on. That gave us a real soaking, but in seconds we were putt-putting safely through the surf line.

Coming back was a different story. Instead of staying behind the breaking wave, we rode over the top and found ourselves surfing. Even though it was not our plan, it was quite exhilarating and would have ended pleasantly had we powered the dinghy straight ahead with the wave. However, the harbor entrance elbowed to the right just past the jetty. When Mac started to make the turn, a wave hit the dinghy sideways with such force that it was pushed up high on its side. We teetered on the brink of flipping over before slamming back on our bottom as the crest of the wave broke over us, filling the Zodiac with seawater. Through it all, the Seagull never faltered. Annie and Joey never said a

The First Life of Andy McCurdy

word, although I suspect they were learning a lesson about what volunteering was all about.

There were no arguments when Mac declared the testing over, and we headed for some hamburgers at the restaurant on the dock. Sitting on the pier with our legs dangling over the edge, we munched our food and admired our new dinghy tied just below.

Then it happened. A twenty-eight-foot Columbia sloop with genoa and mainsail full appeared to be making a downwind approach to our pier. It seemed they were attempting to dock; a maneuver which would require our dinghy to serve as a giant shock absorber if either the sailboat or the pier were to escape serious damage. We realized with horror that our little dinghy was about to explode like a balloon, yet we were helpless to stop it. God only knows why, but at the last second, the boat veered away.

For a second or two I had a chance to make some observations. The guy at the helm of the sloop, (I won't call him the skipper), had a fresh-out-of-a-yachting-store look, complete with a navy blue double-breasted jacket, a captain's hat, a yellow ascot, white flannels and powder blue Topsiders. Everything was new, including the boat. His wife looked equally fashionable, but not so nautical. With a broad-brimmed hat, long pleated skirt and high heels, she looked more suited for a garden party than standing on the foredeck of a sailboat. Completing this dubious crew was one small dachshund, also positioned on the foredeck.

The restaurant district of the harbor was a narrow finger with boat slips defining its perimeter. After just missing us, the Columbia 28 had only a few hundred yards of water before it would run into the closed end of the harbor, where the large fishing boats were tied. Miraculously, instead of crashing there, they managed to turn away and, with the engine on and sails full, they began a second run directly at us. This time I was sure we were doomed, but the gods were with us once again, for at the last second, the sloop somehow managed to swerve away.

The plot thickens, though, for as they pulled away, centrifugal force got the best of the dachshund on the foredeck. With her little legs frozen stiff, she skidded on fully extended toenails across the deck and fell 'plump' into the water. Whereupon the captain's lady began shouting hysterically, "Get Tricksy, get Tricksy!"

Hearing the command, our hero at the helm responded dutifully, but ineptly. If coping with the problems at the helm were not enough, he now attempted a body-over-the-side, one-armed pickup of the dog, sort of cowboy-style. It was a gallant effort, but sadly, too much of our hero got over the side and he did nothing more than join poor Tricksy in the water. When he bubbled to the surface, he saw his boat sailing off without him. He whipped off his glasses and threw them at the cockpit. But, alas, he under threw and they plopped into the water. Perhaps he was just too myopic without them to see the incredible speed with which his craft was leaving him behind.

The Columbia, under no less control with its inept helmsman in the drink, was now on a collision course with a very large yacht tied directly across the harbor from us. The distance was so short that we could see a few people gathered on the yacht's fantail, probably beginning a cocktail hour. Little did they know that they were about two sips away from a serious accident!

"Lets go, Andy! Jump for the dinghy and get that damn engine started!" shouted Mac, who had already hurdled himself toward the bow.

Like Pavlov's dog, I responded automatically and in seconds we were roaring after the sloop. Mac would rescue the damsel in distress by jumping from the dinghy to her boat. However, the timing for this act looked bad, for it appeared that Mac would be aboard the sloop just in time to experience the full impact of walloping into the side of the beautiful seventy-foot yawl. Mac must have felt otherwise for he grabbed the Columbia's starboard shrouds and swung himself onto the deck, as I powered the dinghy around quickly so I would not have to witness the pending calamity at such close range.

At the same time, I got a good view of Tricksy's mistress. Feet well apart, still clad in high heels, she stood on the foredeck, clinging to the head stay and screaming unintelligibly. If it weren't for her unlady-like posture and lack of coherence, she would have fit in nicely with the dignified little cocktail party that she was about to crash.

But, miraculously, it didn't happen. Mac managed to crank the tiller over just in time to miss the yawl by inches. The turning response of the Columbia was impressive, but even more impressive was the far-from-graceful pirouette performed by our lady of the foredeck. With her skirt above her waist, she hung onto the headstay for dear life as centrifugal force shot her right leg straight out directly over the dumbfounded cocktailers, (who, as a group, looked like the most recent addition to Madam Tussaud's Wax Museum). Had it been a planned exercise, our lady's unorthodox salute might have been recorded in yachting history as slightly contemptuous but quite original. Instead, it more resembled the position a full-bladdered Great Dane might assume while watering a fire hydrant.

As I rolled out of my turn, I could see two men in another boat fishing Tricksy and our hero out of the drink, so I turned again to follow Mac. He had already dropped the sails and was motoring for a docking space. We had just reunited when we heard a 'slosh, slosh, slosh' behind us. It was, indeed, the footsteps of our water-logged skipper returning to take command of his yacht. Incredibly, he walked right by without showing us the faintest acknowledgement as he held poor Tricksy so hard that I could see her eyes bulging. He disappeared below deck, leaving us to conjure the epilogue.

And that's what we did, all the way home. We decided that soon we would see a newspaper story reading: "A man, apparently suffering from a bad cold, was arrested on the courthouse steps for inhumane treatment of an animal. He was attempting to strangle a little dachshund named Tricksy when authorities intervened. The man had just responded to several court matters, including a divorce decree, foreclosure papers on his sailboat and a summons for driving a motor vehicle without proper eyeglasses. The beguiling little Tricksy will be placed up for adoption by the Dachshund Rescue League."

Back at the Sumac's christening party, instead of going out for dinner Mom made a special moussaka-type eggplant dish for the regulars. The storytelling that went on kept the tears running down our cheeks, especially Mom's. In the cold light of day she assumed a doubting Thomas role, but when it was time for conviviality, she radiated the very essence of pleasure. The copperish hue of her face, contrasted by her blond hair and green eyes, was stunning, and even though she was my mom, it was on such occasions that I found her elegance overwhelming.

Chapter Three

We were to cast off at dusk, and it seemed that it took the sun forever to sink into the western horizon. Finally, Ruth Winton, our next-door neighbor with the swimming pool, came to round up Joey and Annie. Magnanimously, Ruth had volunteered to take care of them until they would join us in La Paz. I used the time it took to walk the kids to Ruth's car to make a final call to Maggie.

"You guys be good kids. See you in La Paz in a month," I said in a lecturing big-brother tone.

"When the cat's away, the mice will play," said Joey in his infamously smart-ass manner.

I ignored the little monster and dialed Maggie.

"My God," she said. "I just heard the tail end of a news flash. Mexican fishermen reported finding the burnt hull of a sailboat early this morning."

"I know. We got the word a few hours ago. Remember the Wind Song, berthed a few slips down from us... Well, that was the boat, an awful butane accident."

"Maybe not an accident," answered Maggie. "The Coast Guard has called in the F.B.I. I didn't get it all, but something about the brass valves from the stove and oven. They were all turned full on!"

"So you mean that they're suspecting foul play," I asked.

"Maybe. At least they plan to do more investigating," said Maggie.

"Well, I don't know if they want it or not, but they're going to get a lot of help from Mac and Doc. I think they're already planning their own investigation," I added.

"Doesn't surprise me," said Maggie. "Couple glasses of obble gobbles and those two self-appointed detectives would butt into anything... At least its better that they're focusing on solving a crime instead of committing one."

"How true. Well, I just called to say good-bye," I said, changing the subject. "Don't go falling for some brawny football player."

"Don't worry. And you watch out for those dark-eyed senoritas," retorted Maggie.

"Fat chance. Maybe I'll meet a mermaid while I'm diving with Doc in the Sea of Cortez," I joked. "I got to run, Maggie. I already miss you like crazy."

"Same here, Andy. Be a good boy! And, oh, Andy, did you get your hair cut?"

"You know Mexico doesn't allow boys with long hair. So yeah, it's cut short... Looks like hell, too. Love you."

I trotted back to the boat. Mac had the engine running and was looking a bit impatient, so I quickly untied the mooring lines and we were on our way.

At 16:30 hours we cleared Point Loma Light on a southeast heading. Our engine was off and the sails of the Sumac hauled us on a close reach. Two gray whales escorted us as we sailed by the Coronados Islands and entered Mexican waters. The afterglow of a glorious sunset painted the mackerel sky a brilliant red that slowly dimmed to gray, and then finally gave way to darkness. It was my first night at sea and, even though land was only a few miles away, the feeling of separation was enormous. Nothing except our own resourcefulness mattered. I went forward for a few minutes and watched the Sumac's bow propel gracefully through the water. It was reassuring, despite the awesome power of the sea, that our boat seemed sturdy and in harmony with the environment.

Mac called me back to the cockpit as Mom came up from the galley. It was time to review the procedures and safety rules. Mac always said that sailing and flying had a lot in common; they are both very unforgiving of mistakes. Smart sailors practice procedures like spinnaker drill, jibing in heavy seas, reefing the main and changing the head sail at night. According to Mac the most important procedure of all (and possibly the most neglected) is the man overboard drill.

You might expect the greatest danger of a person falling overboard to be when the sea is running high and the crew is being bounced around. Not really, Mac says, because in rough seas people are alert and hanging on. But, during slack time tragedy could quickly strike. A quiet night on watch, the helmsman could decide to "relieve" himself, so with legs braced against the lifeline and weight slightly forward, he lets her go, proud of himself for picking the downwind side of the boat. Just as he is finishing, his body's center of gravity moves slightly seaward. At the same moment the boat can lurch in a counter direction, causing a split second loss of balance, and the crew member is thrown overboard. Mac always interjects that this is not an error limited to male sailors. Women have an even more serious problem in that their peeing posture requires hanging their posteriors way beyond their normal center of balance. Once they were in the water, no one would hear because the combined sounds of the sea, wind, engine and rigging would muffle their screams. In five seconds, the boat could be at least fifty-feet away, and in one minute over six-hundred-feet away.

I thought of how awful it would be to have the next watch and find the boat steering itself and your mate gone! All hands would be called up and a 180 degree back search would commence, but everyone would know that it was a futile exercise. We would think of our friend in the water watching the mast light disappear, then total darkness, panic, and then... What a hideous way to die. We told this story to ourselves because it is true, it does happen. It got us in the mood to seriously practice the man over-board drill.

Mac walked us through the procedure as if he was reading a manual. But, we listened, just like we always listened, even though we knew each step by heart.

"Things should happen almost simultaneously. First the overboard gear should be jettisoned into the water. This consists of a large pole about fifteen-feet long with a weight and flotation device at one end and a yellow or orange flag and strobe light at the other. Attached to the base of the pole is a life-ring. At the instant the gear is cast, the skipper should jibe the boat. In other words, the boat should cross the wind by turning downwind and take a 180-degree reciprocal heading. This maneuver will compensate for the drift of the body in the water. Two crew members should go forward and douse the head sail and, with boat poles in hand, they should commence a starboard and port watch. Engine on, mainsail down, the object then is to converge on the

The First Life of Andy McCurdy

overboard equipment. The person in distress should focus on the flag or strobe light and swim for it, and the forward observers should direct the skipper on a course slightly downwind of the overboard gear. The pickup should be made on the windward side of the boat. A sling should be readied in case the person in the water is injured or the top sides of the boat are too high to pull the person out by hand. The sling should be attached to a head sail halyard, which, in turn, should be rigged to a winch. If the crew acts fast, the odds are that the victim will be saved. If not, the overboard person will probably die by drowning, hypothermia or shark bite."

Mom had brought cabbage rolls for dinner; she and I ate them together while Mac was at the helm. At 20:00 hours, Mom and I started our three-hour watch. We took turns steering on a 155-degree compass heading. It was the first of many, many watches we did together, and I loved them all.

It seemed like no time at all before Mac was on the VHF radio contacting Doc on the Sirius. "This is the Sumac, WRX 2165, calling the Sirius – Do you read?" shouted Mac.

"Roger, Sumac, this is Sirius. Just set our hook in Todos. 23:00 hours and all is well," radioed Doc.

"Got some news on the Wind Song. Investigators found some gas valves in the bilge. They were all turned full open, so maybe something is fishy. Any rate, the F.B.I. is getting in the act – Over," reported Mac.

"That's interesting. Ah, I thought we would visit the lighthouse keeper tomorrow. He might have observed something – Over."

"Go in the morning, better chance he'll be sober. And maybe check with any Ensenada fishermen that are around the island tomorrow – Over," said Mac.

"We're about ten miles northeast of Todos Santos and I'm about to replace Sue and Andy for a three-hour watch. Expect to be anchored in the lee of San Martin before sunset tomorrow night. Will check with you then. This is the Sumac, WRX 2165 – Out," radioed Mac.

The next day at approximately 17:30 hours, true to Mac's prediction, we lowered our anchor behind a rocky point extending from the northeast corner of San Martin Island. It was a snug little spot, perfect in a northwest wind and sea condition.

After reveling in another glorious sunset, darkness fell suddenly. Nothing was visible except the dark outline of the tiny island that protected us and a distant flicker of lights from the mainland village of San Quintin.

Another radio call from the Sirius gave little additional news, except that the light keeper reported seeing nothing the evening of the Wind Song incident.

"Hard to believe," said Doc. "But, then again, by sunset he's totally wasted."

Minutes after the radio call, I headed for the stern cockpit bench with my sleeping bag. As I snuggled in, my thoughts drifted to an early evening last winter. I was watching a sunset with Maggie on Wind and Sea Beach in La Jolla. We were sharing a joint when I told her that God had a shit list and my name was near the top.

When she stopped laughing she said, "Andy, God doesn't have a shit list, but if he did, really bad people would be on it. So what have you done that makes you so bad?"

"That's just it. Outside of dreaming about taking your clothes off, I haven't had a constructive thought in my life. I'm a classic underachiever. I'm a master of how to get by without expending energy. I'm a worry to our parents, and for the life of me, I can't understand why you waste your time with me."

Instead of answering, Maggie rolled on top of me and we passionately embraced until the rising tide nibbling at our bare feet, reminded us of reality; we were overdue for supper.

I would have preferred to dream about Maggie some more, but the excitement of twenty-four hours of sailing and the freshness of the sea air soon brought on a coma-like sleep.

In what seemed like only a moment, I opened my eyes to a very gray daybreak. The Sumac sat calmly, protected by the five-hundred-foot high island, but when I looked south over the sand spit I could see the white caps of a building sea. Mac reported that our anemometer showed thirty knots of wind out of the northwest. I suggested it might be a good day to hole in and practice up on our gin rummy.

For a moment I thought I detected a wait-and-see attitude from Mac, but it never materialized. He said, "Looks like a booming downhill run for us today. We'll reef the main a notch and set a small jib on the head stay."

Hearing no objection from Mom, (her adrenaline had already started to flow), I knew that I had better get my juices moving, too.

After a quick breakfast we secured the contents of our boat for a rough sail, and in minutes, the anchor was up and we powered around the southeast point of San Martin. The mainsail filled and the Sumac steadied down on a broad reach. I hoisted the working jib and, as Mom sheeted her in, Mac shut the engine off. We were already pushing nine knots and we would keep up that speed for the next twenty-four hours. We looked behind us and saw fifteen-foot waves quartering our stern. They were frightening, but we soon realized that our boat could ride up the waves and then surf down the front side. Holding the course required constant effort on the part of the helmsman, and even though an occasional wave would break over our fan deck and drench the cockpit, our confidence in the Sumac soared!

All day and all night we sailed in winds gusting over thirty-five knots. Eating was a chore and there was little chance for sleep, but that was unimportant. The awesome power of the wind and the gigantic size of the sea kept us euphoric. We rarely spoke, and when we did, it was always about our sturdy little boat and how it worked in unison with the forces of nature. Soon we too felt in sync with the mightiness of heavy-wind sailing. Perhaps that is what is meant by getting your sea legs but, beyond that, there was an indescribable, almost spiritual feeling that consumed us.

Our exuberant ocean sleigh ride ended just before dawn. The wind abated as the loom of Cedros Island came into view. By daybreak we were motoring in the calm waters off her east side. The warmth of the sun signaled time to open up the portholes and hatches and dry out the dampness. The wind freshened as we left the lee of Cedros. Soon we were under sail again.

Suddenly, we realized that we had companions nearby. A large gray whale was escorting her calf on an open ocean swim lesson, and the Sumac had become her orientation pylon (so we surmised). She would guide her baby by nudging it in a tight circle around our boat. At times she seemed to almost cradle the little calf on her back, as if to give it rest or, at least, some reassurance. Once or twice the cow broke away from her baby and dove directly under our boat. We could see her tail disappear on one side of the Sumac as her giant head appeared on the other. She sprayed our deck with her spouting exhale and I swear we felt her forty-foot frame lightly scraping our keel. The water show ended abruptly with a tail-out-of-water dive. The mama was probably teaching her fifteen-hundred-pound newborn to sound and swim underwater as they continued a two-hour trip back to their winter home in Scammon's Lagoon. As for us, a two-hour sail would bring us to the quiet protection of Turtle Bay. After having sailed three hundred and fifty nautical miles from San Diego, that was an appealing thought.

Chapter Four

Angel hated Leonard Peters. He was so immaculate, always dressed in a blue suit, sapphire cuff links, red and blue striped tie and a gigantic diamond earring. He was the antithesis of Angel, but she hated him more because he was her boss and treated her subserviently. Most of all, she hated him because he was black.

Five days had passed since the Wind Song caper and it was time to meet Peters for a debriefing. Angel arrived by cab at the San Francisco Airport, had coffee and a chocolate doughnut, then proceeded to the Airporter Inn via shuttle-van.

With minimal amenities, Peters ushered her into his hotel room.

"Start at the beginning, from the moment the pay dirt dinghy arrived in La Paz," said Peters condescendingly.

For the next thirty minutes Angel gave a detailed account, elaborating the gory scene where Bruno slit Tom Bryce's throat from ear to ear. She knew that Peters had a weak stomach for that sort of thing and she relished in seeing him squirm.

"Go back to the beginning. Did anyone see you or Bruno do anything that could connect you to the Bryces?" asked Peters.

"Nobody, except Woogie," answered Angel.

The First Life of Andy McCurdy

"Who the hell is Woogie?" Peters demanded.

"He's my stooge in La Paz. He doesn't have a clue about the hit in Cabo. He only knows what I want him to know," replied Angel nervously.

"So, no stops along the way, no contact with other boats," continued Peters.

"Non-stop all the way to Todos Santos," she lied. Peters would have had a fit if he knew they had stopped in Turtle Bay for fuel.

"There were no possible observers until I met you at the San Diego Airport?" asked Peters.

"Well, a kid saw us for a second on the dock of the San Diego Yacht Club. He wanted to help us fold up the dinghy. It was dark. He didn't see anything. He went back to sleep in the cockpit of a sailboat," answered Angel defensively.

"Then you're not clean. There's a potential witness that saw you three hours after you torched the Bryces," stated Peters.

"So what? Big deal, what's the worry?" said Angel, hoping the subject would pass.

"Maybe not a big deal. But you be damn sure your path never crosses that kid's again – Understand?" said Peters.

"OK, sure," answered Angel. "But it was dark. He couldn't see anything."

"It can't be dark enough to hide Bruno's ugly face. One glimpse of him on a dark night would haunt anyone, especially a kid," said Peters ominously.

"Look, Angel. You're on for one more caper. After that, we're letting things cool off. Do it right and you won't have to work anymore. In about thirty days you and Bruno will be vacationing in La Paz again.

"Your toy, a nice new rubber dinghy, will arrive at an appropriate time. Make no contacts. We'll know where you are and how to make the delivery. You just do your groundwork and follow the plan.

Just act like a couple of tourists. Before you leave for Cabo, see that this Woogie has an accident," ordered Peters.

Angel reviewed the details of the plan with emphasis on contingencies like unexpected encounters or bad weather, especially between Todos Santos and San Diego.

As she was leaving, Peters stood in front of her and said, "One final bit of work, Angel. When it's all over, blow away that idiot, Bruno."

"Don't worry. There won't be a trace of him left," sneered Angel as she went out the door.

On the way back to the hotel, Angel thought about her next caper. Peters always acted like a big shot, but he definitely wasn't the top dog. He answered to some super bigwig that hardly anyone knew about. He was probably a major business guy or maybe a high-level politician: rich, successful and clean as a whistle. 'Just the opposite from me and Bruno,' thought Angel.

They had grown up in the same gang in Watts. Bruno had lived with a worthless, drunken uncle, and Angel lived with her mom in a ratty, old apartment. They got by on what her mom made as a prostitute.

Being the only white kids in a black gang put them at the bottom of the totem pole. They always got the shit detail, and they had to do it right to survive. That included killing an innocent twelve-year-old girl picked randomly by the gang. They did the job or the gang did them. It was just that simple.

Angel had lured the girl into meeting after school one day at a deserted warehouse. The girl was already hooked on drugs, so it took nothing more than asking her to share a joint to convince her to follow Angel. Bruno waited behind a stack of barrels and, as Angel struck a match to give the girl a light, he moved in behind her. With the speed of a cat he drew his knife across her throat, slashing arteries on both sides of her neck. For a moment, the light of the match made the girl's brown eyes shine. She seemed to stare at Angel in disbelief, then slumped to the dirt floor in a pool of blood.

That was a first for Angel and Bruno. The only point of the killing was being able to survive in a miserable jungle.

"Now, after our final caper they want me to waste Bruno. I'd have to think about that. I'd a hell-of-a-lot rather turn the lights off that bastard, Peters," growled Angel to herself.

Chapter Five

Almost completely protected from the raging of the ocean, Turtle Bay harbored a colorful, little village of friendly people. The main enterprise was fishing and anything to do with gleaning from the sea. Adding to the village's color was its very own entrepreneur: the aptly named Gordo. He used to run his business from the beach in front of the village, but some or all parts of his business were eventually deemed questionable (if not illegal). This was only a minor setback for Gordo. He merely moved his operation to a large raft in the middle of the bay. Since selling diesel fuel was the backbone of his business, moving to the raft proved to be a plus. Visiting boats could easily pull alongside and refuel from the fifty-five-gallon drums that Gordo ferried from shore. The biggest problem for buyers was the quality of the diesel – a problem Gordo had brought with him from his operation on the beach. It was anyone's guess where the fuel came from, and no one had a clue as to how old it was. Most visiting yachtsmen had the word on Gordo, and were aware that pouring his fuel directly into a boat's fuel tank could spell disaster. Enough clogged engine stories had trailed back to Kettenburg Boat Yard in San Diego to stimulate some ingenuity. As a result, Kettenburg had invented a stainless-steel box with a nozzle on its bottom that could fit into the deck opening of a fuel tank. The box was divided into three sections, each separated by fine screen. The object was to pump Gordo's lousy fuel into the section of the box farthest from the nozzle, so by the time the fuel worked its way through the screens it would be clean enough to not clog up the engine completely. It was said that, at first, Gordo appeared a bit chagrined about the filters on the decks of visiting yachts but eventually as the money rolled in, he grew quite accustomed to them.

As I said, fuel was the mainstay of Gordo, Inc. His covert activities, however, were even more interesting. "Want some fresh abalone," he would ask. Up went a trap door on the floor of his raft, a quick pull on a rope, and presto, a gunny sack of abs. "Or, do you prefer langouste?" Another rope, another sack, and your wish was fulfilled.

Turtle Bay sported another notorious character: the port captain. Gordo hated him, but he also feared him because the port captain represented the possible end of Gordo's enterprise. "El Capitan" was a dapper little man with a trim mustache. He wore a heavy wool uniform (dreadful attire for a warm climate) with a Sam Brown belt and pistol. In his briefcase, he carried a small inkbox and a stamping block. These objects were obviously his pride and joy, for he loved stamping papers, but not until he had had his whiskey. He liked it served in a small glass at the dining table in the boat's salon. Two small sips and then down went the rest in a gulp. He required two shots before he was ready for business.

That was when we presented the boat's papers, crew list and our visas, and the captain put his stamper to work. With great aplomb, El Capitan pounded his stamping block several times on all papers pushed in front of him. After the ceremony, he shook his head and confided that he was aware of every one of Gordo's unlicensed activities.

Another short one for the road and he stepped off Gordo's raft, into his rowboat, but not before giving poor Gordo a threatening glare. Even though Gordo put on his best hang-dog expression, we surmised that El Capitan was a significant part of Gordo's payroll, and that as long as *mordida* existed, so would Gordo.

After being stamped by El Capitan and refueled by Gordo, we moved the Sumac to a quiet spot where we could swing free on our anchor. Mom was busy making a late breakfast of huevos rancheros. The tantalizing aroma was wafting up from the galley, making me drool at the thought of my first bite. I would roll up a hot tortilla, scoop up a piece of yolky egg, some frijoles and salsa, and bite into a taste sensation beyond compare.

After breakfast, we were all tired but agreed that it was too nice a day for napping, so we loaded up the rubber dinghy with some snacks and headed for a beach on the northeast corner of the bay. Typical of most Mexican beaches, the sand was glistening white and the water was perfect for swimming.

It was not long before the pelicans began an air show. Without a doubt, there are no other pelicans that can dive like the Turtle Bay pelicans! From one-hundred-and-fifty-foot heights, they folded their wings and dropped like rocks into the sea. When they hit the water it looked more like a crash than a dive. You would think the impact would break their necks, or at least knock them cuckoo, but remarkably (after a few seconds to right themselves), they raised their prehistoric bills, and a flopping fish slipped down their gullets. When their feeding time was over, we watched them form squadrons and glide effortlessly just above the water's surface. An hour later, we noticed the pelicans again. They had climbed thousands of feet above us and were obviously enjoying a midday soar. We debated why pelicans were so good at fishing and flying and finally concluded, "Why not, those old birds have had millions of years to practice!"

That night a radio call confirmed that the Sirius had reached Scammon's Lagoon. Doc reported that they had crossed the entrance bar on a high tide and found a deep enough anchoring spot on an inside channel. He suggested that we bring the Sumac over for a rendezvous, but Mac declined. Crossing into Scammon's was risky business for keel boats, and the Sumac had over a foot more draft than the Sirius. That was Mac's excuse, but Doc, (as well as the rest of us), knew that the real reason was that backtracking was not part of Mac's nature.

No one was more goal-oriented than Mac, and Cabo San Lucas was his goal. If it hadn't been for Mom, he would have had us there already. Just sail right through, night and day, that was Mac's way. Fortunately, in matters like this, Mom's way prevailed.

To my delight, an alternate plan developed. In the morning, if calm winds continued, I would take the rubber dinghy back to Scammon's and spend two nights with Doc and Lizzie. They were about thirty miles away as the crow flies, but you had to travel way out and around Punta Eugenia, which made the distance about sixty miles.

Thinking back on it, although I was too dumb to realize it then, my parents must have craved some private time. So unloading me onto Doc and Lizzie must have been subtly prearranged.

The next morning I woke up with the sun and started preparing the Zodiac for my trip. I was totally experienced in small-boat handling, and it was reassuring to know that my parents had no qualms about the plan. Mac checked over the practical stuff like extra gas, drinking water, and a portable radio phone, while Mom boxed up enough food to feed a hungry whale. Then I was on a five-hour sea voyage on my own.

The reliable Seagull purred like a kitten as I rounded Punta Eugenia and headed back east for Scammon's. I spotted white caps on the water about a mile in front of me, and I wondered how this could be when the wind was calm. Then I saw clouds of birds swarming over the turbulent water. Pelicans were dive bombing, and as I drew nearer I could see thousands of gulls, terns and boobies attacking the area, shrieking wildly, grabbing little fish and tearing at pieces of big fish. The water boiled as fish fed upon each other in a total frenzy! Shark, sailfish, marlin, dorado and yellowtail churned the water round me for at least a square mile.

For no good reason, I grabbed a small casting rod and threw a white, single-hooked bone in no particular direction. Before it hit the water, a yellowtail struck. Seconds later, a shark hit the yellowtail. Fortunately that broke my line at the leader, convincing me that trying to fish was a poor idea. In fact, sailing into the center of a serious fish frenzy in a little rubber dinghy was a very poor idea, so I concentrated on steering a straight course through that potentially dangerous phenomenon.

I wondered what in the world ever got the frenzy started. It probably began with a large school of little fish like mullet being chased to the surface by larger fish like sierra that in turn were attacked by bonitos. Then came the dorados, and then the sharks. Small fish were actually jumping into my dinghy! When I finally powered out of the frenzy, I knew that a major shock was in store for Doc and Lizzie – the dinghy and I were both covered with blood and fish debris.

As if that was not enough excitement for a day, in less than one hour I realized that a pod of gray whales was guiding me along the way to Scammon's. Even though they were less than one hundred feet away, I could not tell how many there were. I guessed six, but they swam like a tangled mass of angle worms. The most accurate way I could count them was by watching for spouts. I was worried that every time the whales sounded, they seemed to be surfacing nearer my little dinghy. I calculated that the Zodiac and I collectively weighed about three-hundred pounds, not including the massive lunch Mom had packed, while the whales weighed in at about twenty-thousand pounds each. Obviously, this did not represent a fair encounter. Though I did not fear an attack from my leviathan friends, they did appear curious, and if curiosity turned into playfulness, my dinghy could make a perfect beachball!

It occurred to me that maybe the fish gore covering my dinghy was attracting the whales. Maybe they thought I was a wounded seal and were arguing over who got to swallow me. Then I remembered Doc saying that gray whales don't have teeth. It was probably safe for me to assume that they wouldn't eat a rubber dinghy or a frightened boy. Doc said gray whales eat plankton and other small stuff by straining it through long, baleen fibers that hang down from their upper jaws. I hoped he knew what he was talking about. One thing I knew for sure was that I liked viewing whales a whole lot better from the Sumac than from the little Zodiac. As it turned out, no one ate me. I got a good drenching from their showering exhales, but I soon realized that their only intent was to escort me to the entrance of Scammon's Lagoon.

What a sight I must have made for Doc and Lizzie as they watched my approach through their binoculars. Not only was I splattered with the remains of the fish frenzy, but they had been unable to make radio contact with me as I had neglected to turn on my radio. The latter problem was quickly explained, but the blood and guts were taken more seriously. Naturally, Doc knew all about fish frenzies and, after listening to my story, he began a lecture.

"You know every kind of fish gets involved and they all go crazy, sort of a mob hysteria. Plowing through such a disturbance in a rubber dinghy is not a good idea. Your shape and color make you one of the group... You're not much bigger than some of the marlin and sailfish that were storming through the same melee. Their bills are like sharp spears and one whack, even though inadvertent, could gash a sizable hole in the Zodiac, turning you into a tasty lunch for hungry sharks."

That was enough. Doc's lecture went on but he had already scared the shit out of me. It was time for a quick freshwater shower. The dried spray from the spouting whales had left me smelling like a dead carp.

I had not touched Mom's gigantic food pack, so

the three of us made it our lunch. Afterwards it was time to explore the lagoon.

Locally Scammon's was called Laguna 'ojo de liebra' after a freshwater spring near its eastern border. Doc had anchored the Sirius close to the entrance of the 180-square-mile kidney-shaped lagoon, because navigating inside was difficult. Ribbons of channels went inland for miles, but poor visibility and strong currents made going aground a threat.

Doc's dinghy had a bigger engine, so it wasn't long before we arrived at the east end of the bay. Doc called the whole place a whale sanctuary, but we were now entering the "maternity ward." Our timing was perfect. Less than a mile away we could see clouds of gulls diving into the water.

"Good God, not another fish frenzy," I thought aloud.

But Doc said, "I think we are in luck. A whale might have just given birth and those gulls could be feeding on the afterbirth."

Cautiously, we drew nearer and, sure enough, Doc was right. We couldn't see the actual birth because it happened underwater, but we soon saw the little calf bobbing along on the surface. Unlike its mother, who was covered with barnacles and parasites, the calf's skin was shiny black. Mama was sort of cuddling her baby by rolling on her side. This made her two teats easily available. It did not take long for the calf to start enjoying its first meal. Doc said that mother whales produce about fifty gallons of a rich, buttery milk a day. That sounded like a lot of milk to me, but when I realized that the little calf weighed over fifteen hundred pounds, it started to make sense.

Greeting us as we returned to the Sirius were two ospreys sitting on the yard arm of the main mast. I thought about what great birds they were and what an experience it was for me to be in such consort with nature. Whales obviously took center ring that day, but the birds ran a strong second. We had seen blue herons, plovers, curlews, willets and sand pipers busily scouring the beaches, and pelicans, ospreys and gulls fishing the lagoon from above, just to name a few.

It was cocktail time and Doc offered me a cold beer as the three of us relaxed in the cockpit. When the subject of the Bryce tragedy popped up, it was obvious that Doc and Lizzie had dwelled on the subject much more than we had on the Sumac.

Doc summed things up by saying that he had received a radio call from Ron at the yacht club, and investigators had concluded that foul play was involved. Suicide or an accident was simply not plausible. Three open butane valves from the stove and the ignition key in the off position were substantial clues. Even more ominous was the forensic study done on the partial remains of what was believed to be Rosa's skull. An exit hole was discovered, possibly from a .38-caliber slug.

"How in hell can they do any significant study? I thought there was nothing left but ashes," said Lizzie.

"Forensic work is not down my alley, but..."

Before Doc could finish, Lizzie interrupted with, "In other words, you don't know shit about what happened, and neither does the F.B.I. They mess around with a box of ashes as if they were tea leaves and then conjure up some theory. It's just so much bullshit and it's all paid for by us, the simple-minded taxpayers," said Lizzie as her 151-proof rum cocktail started kicking in.

"OK, throw away the forensic study. The butane valves were open and the ignition switch was off. That's hard evidence that something stinks. Besides, I know Tom Bryce, and there is absolutely no way that he would ever be careless about butane. Absolutely no way," said Doc emphatically.

"So run your theory by us once more, Sherlock," said Lizzie.

Her sarcasm was thick enough that Doc hesitated before answering, "Well, the only logical assumption is that there were intruders that came aboard –either at Cabo, Turtle Bay or Todos Santos – and they intended to use the boat to transport something, probably drugs, into the United States."

"If that's true, why not go all the way into San Diego," I asked in a tone that I hoped would not add to the irritation Lizzie was causing.

"That's easy. Passing the customs dock without reporting is a big risk, and they can't just dock the boat, say good-bye to the Bryces, and be on their merry way without a lot of exposure," explained Doc.

"Remember Mac's first reaction to the accident when we heard about it back in San Diego? He said that maybe pirates attacked them," I said.

Doc seemed to be contemplating my remark when Lizzie spoke up, "I like that one. I can picture our friends, sound asleep when a gang of Mexican banditos, sailing under the good old Jolly Roger sneak onto their boat, cut their heads off, steal all their stuff and torch the boat. Yes, I really like that one. It will make a much more exciting movie."

"As a matter of fact, that's not a bad theory. I lean toward the smuggling explanation, but robbery is a strong contender," conceded Doc.

"So we have two options – smuggling or piracy," I said as a question.

"No, there's one more," said Lizzie, "and that's an accident. I like the pirate version for a movie, but I think they had an accident. Tom and Rosa probably had a rough trip up from Cabo. They're pooped, and finally they have some calm weather. They haven't had sex for over a week, so they pour a touch of tequila, light some candles and romance begins."

"Come on, Liz, the engine ignition was off," explained Doc.

"Sure it's off," said Lizzie. "It's a lot safer to have sex with the engine off. You ought to remember that, Doc."

"Doesn't explain the butane valves being open, though," said Doc as if he were giving in.

"Sure does. Anyone, maybe even you, can get a little careless when they get their wiener up," said Lizzie with a smirk.

"So which way do you vote, Doc?" I asked, thinking it best to derail the direction Lizzie was taking.

"I'm sticking to the smuggler theory. There are a few missing links, but it makes more sense to me. The Wind Song reported in that they were snuggled away in the cove at Todos Santos Island. Early that same evening, even though they had said that they were not leaving until morning, they powered out of the cove and within fifteen minutes the boat disintegrated."

Doc paused for effect, then continued, "That pretty much shoots down the romance theory."

"Why do you say that, Doc," interjected Lizzie.

"Hardly enough time, and if romance was in the air, why not stay in the cove?" answered Doc.

"Don't know about the cove, but fifteen minutes would have been more than enough time if ole rabbit-time Doc had been in the saddle," said Lizzie, thinking she was hilarious.

"Amazing what swigging rum does for your weird sense of humor," burped Doc. "Any rate, the rest is speculation. If the bad guys were robbers, they probably headed back into Mexico. If they were smugglers, they headed for San Diego."

"Two questions, Doc. Why not just blow up the

boat in the cove? And, if their plan was to head for San Diego, why not get the boat a lot closer before they destroy it?" I asked.

"Well, destroying the boat in the cove would make the remains easier to discover. Besides, the explosion might even have awakened the lighthouse keeper from his evening stupor."

"And why not get closer to San Diego?" I asked again.

"Any closer and they risk the Coast Guard spotting the loom of a fire at sea," answered Doc.

"You are a smart son of a bitch, Doc," interrupted Lizzie as she poured another shot of rum over rocks. Her Marine vocabulary was now at full strength, "but you haven't explained how the bad guys made their getaway."

"Well, unless they swam to shore, they had a boat. Maybe one of those seaworthy rubber dinghies or..."

Suddenly, what Doc had just said hit me like a lightning bolt and I blurted out my recollection of the ugly-looking couple deflating their dinghy on the dock the night before we left San Diego.

"Holy shit, Andy, why have you been sitting on that story?" questioned Lizzie.

"I don't know, I just didn't think it was important. Lots of people mess around with dinghies at night at the yacht club, especially on Friday night. To me, they were just a couple of unfriendly visitors. I was glad to be rid of them," I said, feeling a bit stupid.

"Could be just a giant coincidence," said Doc. "But on the other hand, it might be information we should feed back to Ron at the yacht club so he can direct it to the proper authorities."

The conversation drifted from the Bryces to Doc and Lizzie's research in the lagoon: how difficult it was to get an accurate whale count; how much more efficient it would be with an airplane; the problems caused by man indiscriminately invading the sanctuary; what to recommend to prevent such an intrusion.

Then it was evening. I fell asleep on the cockpit bench, but not before gazing at my favorite star, Arcturus. Coyotes on the beach were singing a haunting serenade and, like other recent nights, instead of drifting into sleep thinking of Maggie, that ugly couple kept looming up in my mind.

Why was I haunted by this premonition that somewhere in the not too distant future I would be facing them again? Then it dawned on me that if they really were the Bryces' murderers, and if they were escaping from the crime that night, I might be the only living person who could identify them. That was it. I was a witness, perhaps the only witness that could connect the murderers to the crime.

As I drifted into sleep, my thoughts turned to dreams. I was running down a dark, deserted street and the red-headed woman was chasing me, screaming, "Kill that little son of a bitch!" I could see Mom and Mac way down the street. I tried to catch up with them but my legs turned to rubber. I yelled for help but they couldn't hear me. My words were muffled by torrents of rain and wind and explosions of thunder that followed gigantic streaks of lightning. God was on a rampage. His wrath was upon me. I was doomed.

I woke up shuddering. Arcturus had barely moved so I knew that I had been asleep for only a short time. My dream was still vivid in my mind so I tried not to fall back asleep. My self-confidence was disintegrating and I didn't need any more nightmares. It was bad enough to be haunted by the creepy couple, but now God was after me, too. Maybe my shit list theory was irritating Him. That was my last conscious thought, and then it was dawn.

After a sunrise breakfast we were on our way by dinghy to Puerto Chaparrito, a little village on the north corner of the lagoon. Doc had made arrangements with a local fisherman, Rafael, who owned a Jeep to meet us there and drive us to San Ignacio. Rafael was a very jovial, non-stop talker. His English was a heck of a lot better than our Spanish, but his driving was something else. He seemed to hit every pothole in the road.

We started north on a bumpy trail that lead into Guerrero Negro, the only town of any sorts in the area. After about two hours of getting our tonsils bounced out, we arrived in the small town of El Arco. I was slightly disheartened when Rafael told us that we had gone only forty-five miles and San Ignacio was another seventy-five down the trail. But now we were in the heart of the Baja Desert and the plant life was totally enthralling. Being from California we were accustomed to the common brush like mesquite and palo verde, but now we encountered forests of giant cardon that reminded us of the saguaro found in Arizona. Rafael told us that their trunks are quite sturdy; in fact, in many villages they were used for building beams.

Of all the things we saw that we had never seen before, the oddest of all was the boojums. They resembled warped telephone poles with a few tentacle-like branches that swept in every direction. Together with the boojums, the elephant trees – with their thick trunks and distorted branches – I felt like I was in the forest of the Wicked Witch. I mentioned to Rafael that the elephant tree looked dead, and he explained that they bloom only in June and July when the rain comes. Suddenly, Rafael stopped near an elephant tree and snapped off a twig for us to inspect. He didn't have to ask us to smell it for the aroma of pine was remarkably pungent and lasting. Doc suggested we pack some back to the boat to alleviate the unpleasant odors that have a way of manifesting in hard to vent places.

Lizzie couldn't let that go, saying, "Anything to help rectify the situation after Doc's morning constitutional."

For a moment I thought Rafael's driving had improved, but then I realized the road had firmed into packed sand or adobe and was quite free of potholes. After passing through fields of blue lupine, yellow poppies and purple verbena that carpeted the desert to infinity, we approached the incredible oasis of San Ignacio. In contrast to the dryness of the desert, our eyes were dazzled by the village's succulent greenness. Natural springs irrigated the perhaps one hundred thousand date palms and thousands of orange and other fruit trees that surrounded the village. Narrow little streets lead to a picturesque village plaza that was shaded by an old stand of laurel trees. When I remember my first impression of San Ignacio, (or, for that matter, of Mexico), I think of the profusion of bougainvillea and hibiscus, sprawling everywhere, covering every house, every wall, every building – dazzling us.

Guarding the shady plaza was a remarkably well-preserved mission built by the Jesuits in 1728. Now I'm really not the religious type and my only reoccurring religious thought is that God, probably for good reason, disapproves of me. Even still, the serenity of standing inside the mission really got to me. It wasn't a pious feeling, but I was overwhelmed by the natural beauty of the stone structure that had been built hundreds of years ago in the middle of nowhere. What a testimony, not only to the devotion and sensitivity of the early padres, but to the generations of villagers whose constant efforts have preserved that historical structure.

It was a long, bouncy return trip to Scammon's Lagoon. We were back aboard the Sirius by sunset, tired, but filled with memories of the incredible Baja desert. After supper I retreated to the fantail and fell into a dream-free, knockout sleep. I did not hear the coyotes, or anything else for that matter, until daybreak.

Mac wanted me to leave early for two reasons: the winds would be calm enough for a dinghy trip, and he was antsy to start another leg south by early afternoon. Breakfast was followed by some last minute instructions from Doc. He repeatedly told me to avoid all fish frenzies. Then I got a big hug from Lizzie, which I did not mind at all.

On the way back to Turtle Bay I started thinking about where I was in life, and why I got excited over a hug from Lizzie. But, like I've said before, even though she was at least Mom's age, she was warm and had big breasts. I guess that was consistent with the disgusting quality of my character. No wonder God disapproved of me. No wonder I was nothing but a worry to my parents. I could not get a hug from an old friend without getting worked up and, of course, I was shocking the world because I was in love with my stepsister. I tried to forgive myself because I was only sixteen and about every ten seconds I had thoughts that gave me a hard on. I was surely near the top of God's shit list. I was probably due for a dreadful day of reckoning at any moment, unless there was some truth to what I had once heard Mac say.

Mac said God is way too busy to be worried about one little insignificant person. Problems, like keeping the stars from crashing into each other or keeping gravity from shutting down, keep the Old Guy totally occupied. Mac thinks that the people who get down on their knees and ask God to solve their problems would do better standing up and working out their own damn problems.

Mac always says, "Don't tell people your problems – half the people are not listening, and the other half think you got just about what you had coming to you."

But Mac has it all worked out, and he's old and settled and he doesn't do much wrong, except maybe drink too many obble gobbles with Doc. But me, I was a goofed-up kid with runaway hormones. I'd have been a damn fool to bank on God being too busy to take a second away from gravity to fire a lightning bolt through my head, quickly ridding the world of an irresponsible pest. Probably the fish frenzy a couple days ago was a setup for a marlin to spear me through the heart, but God got sidetracked by some problem in the universe. But enough with the self-flagellation, I wasn't even seventeen. There was plenty of time to develop character. Besides, it was much more soothing to spend the four-hour trip back to the Sumac dreaming about Maggie.

A black cloud on the horizon snapped me out of my daydreams. What the hell was it? Maybe God

The First Life of Andy McCurdy

had thrown a lightning bolt at me and missed! The cloud kept coming nearer; it seemed to be heading for Turtle Bay. I thought that it was a boat with a really bad fire aboard, but as I drew closer I couldn't see any flames, just dark, black smoke. Finally, at the entrance of the bay, I saw a sight that made me rub my eyes in disbelief. It was an old, one-hundred-foot long, steam-driven side-wheeler coming out of the ocean as if she were on the Mississippi one hundred years ago. Smoke bellowed out of her giant stack as her pilot threw her into reverse to set the anchor. It was the Eppleton Hall, and I soon learned that she was not a Mississippi riverboat. Instead, she had been built in England in 1914 to tow coal barges on the River Tyne. Fifty years later, she was sold for scrap and left to rot on a mud bank; but fortunately, some enterprising souls had brought her back to life. Now, three years later, the Eppleton Hall had nearly completed a miraculous voyage! She had steamed across the Atlantic and into the Pacific, via the Panama Canal, and was taking a brief rest in Turtle Bay before continuing her epic journey to San Francisco where she would rest in the Maritime National Historical Park.

Chapter Six

Mac was chomping at the bit when I pulled up alongside the Sumac. In ten minutes he had the dinghy stowed and we were set for the open ocean. As we sailed out of Turtle Bay, Mac and Mom listened to my tales of the whale birthing and the Baja desert. That got us talking about the natural beauty and tranquility of the whole area, and we wondered if such a special place would remain unspoiled. Being isolated was a positive factor, but the invasive tentacles of developers are far-reaching and the silly notion of leaving such a beautiful place untouched was beyond their comprehension.

Mom had a few pet peeves, and the haughty "we know what's best" attitude of land developers, particularly the ones that specialize in concreting over pristine little places in the wilderness, just might top her list.

"They are so deluded by big bucks that they actually believe their pretentious towers and golf courses improve the area," moaned Mom.

Mac agreed, but he dismissed the developers of wilderness sanctuaries as invading profiteers and let it go at that. He saved his energy to come down on do-gooders, especially those who run around in remote places pounding their religion and lifestyle down the throats of folks that seem perfectly content with their own beliefs. Mac and Mom always fed off each other during those rantings, so I just sat back and listened.

We were rested and ready for the sea again. The wind god was good to us, providing a steady sixteen-knot breeze out of the west. Typically, when conditions were so comfortable we would sit around and philosophize, but this time we fished.

Our technique was a bit lackadaisical. We trailed a red and white feathered lure from a hefty fishing rod that we placed in a makeshift rod holder off our stern. Because watching the fishing line was a low priority, we tied a light monofilament line to the fish line beyond the rod and ran the other end back to the ship's bell in the cockpit, thus making a fairly effective fish alarm.

Shortly after a late lunch, we were all feeling lazy (Mom and Mac were talked out), when the bell started clanging away wildly! The sound startled us and its significance did not immediately penetrate our sleepy minds. Mom reacted first, for she was steering the boat. She grabbed the rod and tightened down the drag, but the fish was unstoppable – partially because the boat was moving seven knots in the opposite direction. Mac swung the Sumac up into the wind causing the sails to luff and the boat speed to drop. As we angled back toward the fish, Mom was able to put some line back on the reel. A good thing, for there was over four hundred feet of line in the water. Suddenly the fish made his first appearance. A dorado in the forty-pound range soared ten feet straight into the air and, then, with a series of greyhound-like leaps, streaked across the water. With ease, he took back all the line Mom had retrieved and then some. For the next half hour he was totally in charge; stripping out one hundred yards of line at will – then, instantly reversing his direction, he would charge the boat with such speed that it was impossible to retrieve the line fast enough.

With each leap the afternoon sun intensified his brilliant colors of gold and emerald green. We had never seen a fish put on such a spectacular display, but eventually he tired and we were able to bring him under our stern. Mac reached down with a baseball-like bat with a gaffing hook at its end, and snared him out of the water and onto our fantail. Had it not been for the excitement of the battle, we might well have thought to release him. Instead, we watched his brilliant colors quickly dissipate as he grew lifeless. Even though we have caught many fish since then without feelings of remorse, and even though we enjoyed many superb meals from that catch, there had been a magnificence about that dorado that left us with regret.

Just after sunset, Mac made radio contact with the Sirius on our single sideband. Doc had been in contact with Ron back at the yacht club. A very interesting development had surfaced. John Swingler, owner and skipper of the Lobo del Mar, had watched the Wind Song depart from Cabo San Lucas. In fact, as he received a good-bye wave from Tom Bryce, John had snapped a photo of their departure. Later, after studying the photo, it appeared to John that something was sprawled on the deck house of the Wind Song. He had the picture enlarged and the results clearly showed that it was a deflated dinghy. That was very strange, because the Bryces only carried one dinghy and the picture showed it hanging on the Wind Song's stern davits. Even more ominous was that the enlargement showed a form in the companionway between the cockpit and the main cabin. Quite possibly the form was another person keeping the helmsmen under surveillance.

Suddenly theories were narrowing in on some possible conclusions. The Bryces' killer, or killers, must have confronted them in Cabo San Lucas and must have brought along their own rubber dinghy. Those assumptions now seemed credible, and they just upgraded my evening encounter with the couple on the dock to more than just an unrelated coincidence.

"Tell us the story once more, Andy," asked Mac.

Again, I tried to answer the usual barrage of questions. "No, I didn't see where they went. No, I did not see a car, in fact I'm not even sure if they were inflating or deflating their dinghy."

"That's my point, Andy. You had a brief run-in with a couple on the dock. That's about it, except it happened around three hours after the Bryces' death – to make more out of it seems like a real stretch to me."

"Well, that's easy for you to say, Mac. But if that ugly couple really are the killers, then I'm the fly in the ointment to them."

"What do you mean?" questioned Mac.

"Stop and think about it. I'm a witness, maybe the only witness that actually saw them as they left the crime scene. Maybe they've forgotten all about me, but if they really are the killers, I doubt it. They'll remember the kid on the dock, and if that kid were to drop dead, that wouldn't disappointment them at all."

"Holy cow, Andy. If I didn't know better, I'd worry that you were back on a La Jolla beach smoking pot with Maggie."

That really pissed me off. Not just the pot insinuation – I wondered how the hell he knew – but the fact that Mac gave a lot less credence to my story than Doc did.

I was about to challenge him but he abruptly changed the subject by saying, "Who's standing first watch?"

Mom was tired, so I volunteered to take the early watch alone. Mac stayed up with me for a while even though there was no need. It was a quiet evening with a steady, reaching breeze and little for the helmsman to do but steer a straight course.

I didn't want to talk about the slimy couple anymore, but I was glad Mac was staying up. It gave me a chance to entice another Korean War story out of him.

"So, anyway," Mac's story began with the usual preamble, "one night at K2 air base, the usual gathering of pilots at the officers' club was generating a head of steam. Stimulated by twenty-cent drinks, the songs were getting louder and raunchier by the round. 'When the Ice Is Off the Rice Across the Yalu' and 'I Love My Wife' were usually followed by a few passionate toasts to missing comrades, which led to the smashing of empty glasses on the concrete floor. Sometimes the broken glass got to be ankle deep, particularly during an extremely long and energetic party."

I asked Mac what determined an ordinary party from a real smash-a-roo.

"Really nothing in particular, other than there not having been one for a while," and then he continued:

"So there was a real fandango going on this particular night. Glasses were flying in all directions.

The First Life of Andy McCurdy

Someone would drink a toast and off went another volley. Crushed beer cans were clamped to the bottom of boots so deafening noise could be made by foot stamping. This party was really out of control and, like a raging fire, nothing but time was going to stop it. Except this one time, Colonel Nelson did it all by himself.

"Now the Colonel had nothing against parties. In fact, he participated in most of them, but he seemed to have a sixth sense that told him when slipping out the side door would be the appropriate move. After all, he was in command of three fighter squadrons made up of about sixty young pilots and almost all of them were dancing around the concrete floor, blowing off steam like only a bunch of twenty-four-year-old fighter pilots could do.

"To any other group in the world, the frenzy of such behavior would be way beyond their comprehension, but to the pilots of the 58th Fighter Bomber Group, it was just another Tuesday night," related Mac.

"But, when Colonel Nelson, and only Colonel Nelson, walked out in the middle of the floor and raised his hands above his head and shouted, 'At ease!', the volume dropped instantly and a ragtag bunch of boys stood bleary-eyed, but quiet.

"'I hate to break up a good party, boys, but orders have just come in from 5th Air Force Headquarters. The 310th squadron will be temporarily evacuated from this base and will relocate to an unoccupied airfield a few miles south of Seoul. There are no facilities there, so all supplies to make you self-sufficient will be airlifted. C119s from Japan will be landing here momentarily. All 310th pilots pack your toothbrushes, dress for flight and report to the flight operations shack immediately. All pilots from the 311th and 474th are on alert. Report to your barracks. The party is over,' barked the Colonel."

Mac said that the next thing he remembered was following my dad who, in turn, was following a single line of pilots. The lead guy had a flashlight and the rest were stumbling along behind.

"That was the only way we could navigate the three hundred yards back to our barracks because the ground fog was so thick. It was not a great night for flying.

"You know when I think back on it, I wonder how in hell twenty young men could pull themselves out of a party stupor and prepare to fly jet fighters. But then I remember that these were unique people with rare qualities, almost as if they had a built-in switch: off – they went into the party mode; and on – the shoulders went back and jaws set with the take-no-shit attitude of a fighter pilot. Medical science might not agree, but with the immediate help of some black coffee and, once in the cockpit, more help from a few deep inhales of pure oxygen, heads were clear and all systems were go," recalled Mac.

"Try to pick those kids out of a crowd and you wouldn't have much luck – fighter pilots have no apparent norm. Their common denominators are all internal. They thrive on the excitement of their jobs and can unflinchingly look death in the face with a smile. It's not that they are immune to fear – that would be abnormal – but they know how to control their fear so it does not interfere with the precision demanded when they are under incredible stress.

"So, by the time we climbed into survival suits and strapped on parachutes, the fog had settled in like pea soup. Two Jeeps were parked on each side of the runway. Headlights on, their purpose was to define the starting spot for take-off. One at a time we taxied our F-84 Thunderjets between the Jeeps, then locked our brakes, set the directional gyro to zero, pushed the throttle full forward to let the engine wind up to one-hundred-percent power, then released the brakes and commenced an instrument take-off. We'd brake to steer until speed built allowing rudder control, then came the incredible feeling of acceleration as your body was forced back against the ejection seat. Eyes were glued to the directional gyro, zero degrees tolerance to stay on the runway. Constant cross-check with the airspeed indicator and, when the needle crossed 130 knots, back pressure on the stick, nose wheel off the ground as the flight indicator and altimeter become part of the cross-check. Airborne, gear up, add the rate of climb indicator to the cross-check. Gain speed, milk up the flaps, more speed, gentle back pressure on the stick and start a soaring climb. Concentrate, direction indicator, rate of climb indicator, airspeed, altimeter – concentrate! Twenty seconds later and 'boom' you exploded out of the fog and into a starry sky. Eyeballs out of the cockpit for the first time since you started your take-off roll, start a slow climbing turn to the right and spot your flight leader, then turn hard right and join up on his wing. Within thirty seconds, a second element of two Thunderjets joined the formation and we proceeded to climb north as a unit of four."

Listening to Mac relive his experiences was entrancing. I would forget that I was at the helm of Sumac but it was not a serious problem even though we were straying all over the ocean. 'Harder to get in trouble going six knots than six hundred,' I thought to myself.

"Well, what was the point of the evacuation," I asked.

"A mobility exercise," said Mac. "As if we didn't have enough to do flying missions and partying, front office brass would dream up hypothetical situations, and this one was a lulu. Remarkably, by sunrise our squadron was totally operational off an old abandoned airfield. In fact that morning, your dad and I flew a reconnaissance mission across the 38th parallel. Like everyone else, we hadn't slept a wink and were taking bennies to function. On the way back, your dad, who had incredible eyesight, spotted a North Korean truck convoy.

"I remember him saying, 'are we all drugged up or do I see live targets?'"

Mac continued, "We were at twenty thousand feet above broken layers of cumulus clouds, so it was a miracle that Andy spotted them. Even more remarkable was that they were there at all. North Korean convoys almost always moved at night. No doubt, there was something urgent in their mission, for they were all bunched up and traveling fast, leaving a tell-tale cloud of dust behind them. In short, they were a classic dream target for a couple of fighter pilots.

"We were behind them heading south so they wouldn't see or hear us until it was too late. Andy started a steep dive as I maneuvered to get sufficient space behind him. At about eight thousand feet we broke out of the clouds, and an instant later they were in our gun sights. Andy concentrated on the front trucks and I bored in on the rear ones. Suddenly, some of the lead trucks exploded into balls of flame. They were obviously carrying munitions, because the concussion from Andy's hits buffeted my plane as if I was flying into a thunderstorm. Andy initiated a tight chandelle turn to the right, so I joined up on his wing as we both prepared for a second run. As we gained altitude, we saw fires and explosions like a gigantic fireworks display that had miscued and ignited simultaneously.

"The lead truck was still intact and running for cover but there was none available. Andy timed a diving turn perfectly, pulling out about thirty feet above the road and a few hundred yards behind the truck. In seconds, his .50-caliber shells were ripping the truck apart. Then just as he passed over it, the truck exploded. The smoke momentarily obscured my vision, and for a second, I thought the concussion had gotten your dad. But soon he joined on my wing as we assessed the damage. Except for one, all the trucks were completely destroyed. We observed only burning wreckage, with no apparent survivors. The back truck, though, might have been carrying personnel instead of munitions, for although it sustained a few hits, it was still intact along the side of the road.

"Then Andy noticed that the tarp covering the truck bed had been dropped; they were probably carrying an anti-aircraft weapon, like a quad 50, and they had it readied in case we attacked again. We certainly didn't want to disappoint them, so with me on your dad's wing, we climbed toward the morning sun, then reversed our course and dove out of the sun at the remaining target.

"We guessed correctly. They did have fire power but their tracers were showing above us. They had misjudged our angle of attack. Our speed and the glaring sun hampered their ability to sight, and they only had a couple seconds to aim right. Unfortunately for them, they were wrong. They received the devastation of our blazing .50-caliber machine guns. We circled once to survey the damage and concluded that there was no need for a third strike. It was sure that some North Korean fortification would be a tad short of ammunition that night.

"By late afternoon, every pilot had flown at least two missions. Then some genius from above called the alert over. We were told to stand down and get some rest until further orders came. Well, try taking a nap after you've had a few bennies. We were so wound-up that our eyelids were frozen open.

But, never fear, just about the time a mounting fatigue hit us, orders came in declaring the operation a great success and all pilots should immediately prepare for the flight back to K2. It was still daylight and the weather was clear, so with the remnants of our energy we found our way home. That night there was no party at the club," Mac concluded.

Eventually, Mom appeared for watch. Mac insisted he was not tired, so I left the two of them and took some sack time. But dreams of flying a fighter gave way to my new obsession: that dreadful couple on the dock. The premonition that I was destined for another encounter with them was growing into a real horror. Finally I got my mind to visit a more relaxing subject: walking on the beach, hand-in-hand, with Maggie. Deep sleep soon came.

Chapter Seven

By mid-afternoon the next day the wind had freshened to twenty-five knots, giving us beautiful surf rides down some large waves. I was at the helm, concentrating on steering a downwind course to avoid an accidental jibe. As we pulled up high on the crest of a large swell, I saw an object not three hundred feet off our starboard bow. Mom, who was on the foredeck tightening the topping lift, saw it too.

She yelled at me, "Head up, Andy!"

The wind dumped out of the sails, causing a whipping, snapping luff that brought Mac on deck from his little siesta. He and Mom sheeted in the sails enough to diminish the luffing and maintain our headway as we neared what appeared to be a skiff awash. She was painted glossy blue and yellow and had about a 35-horse outboard on her transom. As we passed downwind, we could see that the skiff also carried a Briggs and Straten air compressor and was fully rigged for abalone and lobster diving.

Mac shouted, "Let's dump the spinnaker fast!"

This was a maneuver we had down pat. Mom took the helm and held the course directly downwind as Mac uncleated the spinnaker halyard and motioned to Mom to head down even more, putting us on the verge of a jibe. At the same time, I slacked off the afterguy, allowing the spinnaker pole to shoot forward to the head stay. This action blanketed the spinnaker behind the mainsail, causing it to dump its wind. Mac took the wraps off the halyard winch and the spinnaker started dropping fast. Working my arms like a windmill, I hauled in the giant sail from the leeward side of the Sumac as Mom pointed our bow up into the wind. Mac secured the spinnaker pole to the foredeck, cleaned up the halyard and afterguy, and then ran back to the cockpit to help me complete the haul in. The job was completed flawlessly as the Sumac, powered by its mainsail alone, continued to roar down the back sides of giant waves at speeds above eight knots, with a side-to-side roll so steep that a river of seawater washed over the cap rails, flooding the decks and drenching the cockpit. This wasn't a problem though, because our little crew had performed a delicate maneuver with speed and precision comparable to an eight-man professional racing crew. There was no time to savor a job well done, because we had to battle our way upwind to reestablish contact with the twenty-foot skiff that was awash and showing no sign of life aboard her.

 The sailing brake was pulled off to free the propeller shaft as our diesel engine belched out its customary cloud of start-up smoke. With the mainsail hauled in close, we started to motor-sail against six-foot waves that broke over our windward bow. Although the spinnaker drop took only a few minutes, it would take us at least half an hour to beat back to where we last saw the skiff. That was more than enough time to convince me that sailing downwind was a great deal more pleasant than crashing headlong into the waves and wind. Mac ordered out the foul-weather gear. We suited up in our yellow, waterproof pants and jackets and strapped on our safety harnesses. That should have been done sooner, because we were already soaked.

As I took a lookout position by the main mast, I wondered, even if we do get back to the skiff, what could we possibly do with it?

I hadn't pondered that question for long when Mac shouted for me to come back to the cockpit. "We have some alternatives here, but there is no way we can bring her aboard."

As much as I appreciated Mac's judgment and ability, I really thought that his conclusion was obvious to even the most casual observer. The skiff was big and heavy, and full of tons of water.

"Probably too dangerous in this sea to drop someone into her. Besides, she's awash in breaking waves – no way you could get ahead bailing."

That particular alternative grabbed my attention. The candidate for such an act was certainly not Mac; he was needed at the helm. It wouldn't be Mom either; she was too useful, and besides, she's Mac's wife. But me, who was at the top of God's shit list and a total nuisance to the world... Well, what was the loss if things didn't go well?

I knew I could count on Mom to veto dropping me into the skiff, but it was still a plan that had to be squelched before it even got to a vote. I started listing all the reasons why it wouldn't work, with the most obvious being that I was already in a state of panic over the thought of it!

But before I got on a roll, Mac interrupted in a sort of "now hear this" tone, "We can take her in tow. When we get up close, Andy, snare her painter with the boat hook, hand the line to Mom and she'll tie it to our port dock cleat. I'll hold the Sumac into the wind, and as soon as the line is secure we'll fall off to starboard. When Mom takes the line you get ready to let out the mainsail so we can get back on a downwind run again."

"Before we begin this asinine maneuver, would

you have time to answer a question or two, Capitan?" Mom asked. She didn't wait for an answer. "Why are we doing this?"

"The skiff is a hazard to navigation, so we should do our best to correct the problem," Mac replied.

"For crying in the beer, so we have to risk our lives to rid the ocean of all foreign objects? I think you've got your greedy little eyes on that air compressor and outboard engine," argued Mom.

Mac, showing no sign of wavering, snapped, "We haven't got time to argue. We have to make a try at this!"

The debate ended for good as I shouted, "Dinghy dead ahead! Dinghy at twelve o'clock!"

Coming upwind on her, the skiff looked bigger. We were getting close. I readied myself with the boat hook on the port side, and Mom stood aft of me, ready to grab the skiff's painter. Our safety harnesses were snapped onto the lifelines in case we fell overboard. Mac reduced our engine power and headed up enough to luff the mainsail. As the Sumac lost speed, we started to "hobby horse" in the sea. Wave after wave took our boat high into the air. As a huge wave slid by, we were momentarily suspended, only to come crashing down on the water with such impact that our boat was jarred from the tip of her mast to her keel.

Then we were alongside the skiff and I moved to snag her painter, but I hesitated. There were two lines hanging off her bow: one was orange, the other yellow.

Mac shouted, "Grab it, Andy!" He couldn't see that I had a decision to make.

I went for the yellow rope because it looked as if it was secured to the skiff's bow pad. As the boat hook caught the line, I swung the pole back to Mom. There was enough slack so that she could debate. If the circumstances were different, and there were time for discussion, the Sumac would become a floating democracy. On rare occasion, even I had a say. More often than not, Mom's position prevailed. My record-keeping clearly indicated that Mom had a four-to-one chance of getting her way.

So there we were, powering upwind again after that glossy blue and yellow skiff. I found myself praying for our safety as we continued risking our lives for the general safety of all mariners at sea. Then I realized that I was being foolish: if, by any diminutive chance, my praying distracted God from His major task of gravity tending, He might seize the moment as an excellent opportunity to polish me off for good!

Mac announced, "We'll pass her to windward this time. We'll have our low side toward the skiff – much easier to grab her."

I mentioned to Mac that I had seen two lines over the bow of the skiff. He had noticed them, too, and told me that the yellow one was an anchor line. He paused for a moment, then asked, "Did you notice anything else in the water?"

I shook my head, "Only the other line, the orange one, the one that looks like a diver's safety line... Do you think...?"

Mac's grim expression answered my question. When a line from a drifting boat hangs deep and taut in the water, it is a fair assumption that there is a weight of some kind on the other end. To assume that this weight could be a dead body was not a stretch. The blue and yellow skiff was rigged to dive for abalone and lobster. It carried two lines off its bow: one for the anchor, and the other for the diver. The diver's line was normally orange.

The reality of what might be revealed if the rescue was successful struck unsettlingly in the pit of grab the line and run it back to the aft cleat. But before she could secure it, we realized that we had overstayed our time and were dangerously close to another floating object. A nasty wave crested under us, pushing our bow enough off the wind to allow a wind gust to catch our mainsail and heel us over to the starboard. Simultaneously, the wave slammed the skiff against our exposed bottom. The impact knocked Mom and me off our feet but we fell into the sail. We were shaken, but unhurt.

Brave old Mom. Through it all she never let go of the painter. It was still slack as we started to sail away from the skiff. Mom quickly threw the line back to Mac who cleated it a second before it drew out stiff. We were crosswise to the ocean waves now and rolling from side to side so steeply that all we could do was hang on for dear life. Just as we appeared to be making a more comfortable downwind course, the skiff started to submarine. The added stress instantly snapped the yellow line, causing it to whip over our heads with a frightening crack, setting us back where we were thirty minutes before.

At once, a serious discussion broke out between Mom and Mac as to the merits of continuing this chore.

"We might have already damaged our boat, and two of us were almost tossed overboard. What's the point? We'll just add to the debris already in the sea," pleaded Mom.

Mac still contended that an object awash was a hazard to others and stood firm. Surprisingly, Mom relented. What a disappointment. I would have bet all my marbles that we were totally and completely through with that skiff forever!

There was no question that Mac was the captain of the Sumac. He was a knowledgeable sailor and called all the shots when there was no time for my stomach. Again, but this time more desperately, I found myself praying that the mission would be aborted. My prayers would again go unanswered. Mac had sighted the skiff and barked out a general call to battle stations.

"Get the boat hook ready, Andy. We'll pass her to windward with a little more speed this time. Get the line back to Mom so we can turn downwind!"

Now the skiff was dead ahead. I screamed, because it looked like Mac was going to drive our bow right into her. At the last second he swung the Sumac hard into the wind. We glided beside the skiff so close that I could grab the lines with my hands. The sea calmed momentarily as I handed the lines to Mom, who ran them back to Mac. He secured them and gave the Sumac full right rudder. The bow pulled off the wind sharply. The mainsail filled and Mom let the sail run out until we were on a relatively stable broad reach.

The skiff fell back into a tow position, but before we could congratulate ourselves on our mission accomplished, the horror we had imagined struck. The tail end of the orange line surfaced. Tied to it was a man's body. He wore a short-sleeved wet-jacket, and the line was secured to a dive belt around his middle. The body began to plane, then went into a slow, pinwheel-like spin as its arms and legs flopped like rubber tentacles.

Suddenly a cresting wave lifted the skiff and its dead owner so high above the Sumac that, had the wave broken at that precise moment, the stern of our boat would have been smashed. Instead, the wave carried forward and broke directly astern, surging its water over our transom and filling the cockpit and spurting down the companionway, drenching the main salon. At the same time, the skiff submerged into the back side of the wave with such force that it probably found the ocean's floor.

Its towline snapped like a thread, and that was the last we ever saw of that fucking skiff!

For one glorious moment I thought the excitement was over. The three of us untangled ourselves from each other on the cockpit floor, which now resembled a saltwater bathtub. Without a helmsman, the Sumac had sailed directly downwind. As we slid down the next wave, she started to round up toward the other tack.

Mac shouted, "Jibe! Duck everyone," as he fought to regain the helm.

But it was too late for me. I was standing on the port deck when the wind filled the mainsail on its back side, causing the boom to swing at me like a falling oak tree. I must have rolled slightly away as the boom struck me full force on the right shoulder.

As I flipped over the side, I asked myself, 'why didn't it hit me on the head? I'd be dead now, which was infinitely better off than bobbing around in a cold sea, waiting to drown.'

I hit the water, and my body took another jolt. How could a shark find me so quickly? Then I remembered the thirty-foot lead line securing my safety harness to one of the lifelines on the Sumac's deck. The second after I hit the water, the line went taut and I was off on a tow ride. Somehow that damned cadaver had stayed attached through the wave incident and was engaging me in a water ballet that could only amuse Charles Addams. Pulpy arms and legs were slapping me, and as its body continued to pirouette, centrifugal force flipped its head toward mine. The dead man's mouth was open and his buckteeth struck into my cheek. I felt no pain, but blood gushed from a substantial gash. All of this was incidental to the total revulsion I felt.

I was paralyzed with terror and only sensed the roaring sound of water as I struggled to be free of my lifeline so I could drown alone. But instead, the tow lines twisted tighter, locking me into that rotting, bloated corpse like it was my Siamese twin.

'Oh, God, help me, please,' I prayed.

The whole episode took only seconds. Mac slowed the boat in preparation to winch me in. The next thing I saw was Mac as he reached down for me with the fish gaffing bat. I remembered thinking that there must be a more dignified way to bring me aboard, but being gaffed was consistent with the rest of my recent luck and far less terrorizing than my duet with the cadaver.

Mac missed my stomach with the gaff by a fraction of an inch, setting the hook onto my safety harness. Then, with my arms and legs flailing, Mom and Mac grabbed a piece of me and we fell as one into the cockpit.

Mac didn't wait to share a reunion hug. Instead, with boat-knife in hand, he jumped to his feet and slashed the orange line, releasing forever the remains of the Mexican fisherman. I found out later that, just as I was extracted from the sea, two medium-sized sharks struck the cadaver, ripping both his legs off.

It would not have mattered if I had known at the time; my emotional meter was already maxed out and I could hardly comprehend what had happened. I just sat in the cockpit with my head buried in my mom's lap and bawled. I don't remember how long I stayed there with my arms wrapped around her waist. Except for sobbing, I don't remember anything – not even the bandage being placed over the bone-deep gash on my cheek where that shithead had bitten me.

It was almost dark when I finally withdrew from my mother's womb and once more entered the world of the living. The wind was calmer and we were moving under engine power. I saw a beacon light off our port bow. Mac told me it was Cabo San Lazaro.

As the three of us sat on the cockpit bench together, I wondered if my legs could get me down to the head. When I stood up, Mom and Mac jumped up to steady me. We almost ended up as a tangle on the cockpit floor again. Instead, we just stood there for a moment. No one said anything; we just held onto each other.

When I came out of the head, I felt a little better. It was gratifying to have taken inventory of my body and found nothing missing – just a few bumps and bruises. Mom greeted me with hot broth laced with a touch of *anejos*. My mouth was a cottonball but slowly my tastebuds opened. The soup became palatable and the rum stimulated a slight revival.

I stood behind the wheel with Mac. He put his arm around me and said, "I put out a radio position report on where we last saw that skiff. I guess we broke it up enough so it won't be a danger to another boat."

I didn't say anything, but wondered if Mac was attempting to lighten the load with a touch of humor, or if his insatiable optimism was seeking a fleck of purpose for engaging us in the extraordinary events of the afternoon.

I tried to focus my eyes on the San Lazaro Light which was almost abeam our port side, but it kept dancing around like it was trying to join the stars in the sky. My legs were like rubber and I suddenly felt tired, more tired than I had ever felt in my life. That's all I remember. The worst day of my life was over.

Chapter Eight

I spent the night on the quarter berth, directly across from the galley. I must have slept like the dead, because I never heard a sound, even when Mom had been busy making a huge omelet breakfast just feet from my head. My face ached where that sodden cadaver had sunk his buckteeth into my cheek, and when I tried to move my right arm to inspect some body parts, a paralyzing pain shot down my shoulder to my fingertips.

It was some sort of a miracle to have survived being whacked by the giant mainsail boom of a fifty-foot sloop, not to mention the water events that followed. I remembered thanking God just before I had fallen into a deep sleep. True, it was a slight departure from the 'God is too busy tending to gravity' theory espoused by Mac, but the fact was that I did survive. I was not crushed by a jibing boom, nor was I eaten by a dead fisherman or a hungry shark, and I did not drown. Who else was there to thank but God?

The aroma of bacon and eggs got me up and I limped to the table, surprised by my hunger. The breakfast conversation ranged from subdued to non-existent, until Mac looked at me with what appeared to be watery eyes, and said, "Andy, I'm sorry."

I had never heard such words from a parent. I mean, we kids are perpetually saying that we are sorry, but adults don't say that kind of thing to kids – never.

Then he went on to say, "I really blew it. I risked the lives of two people that I love dearly, and for what? There's no excuse – I'm ashamed."

"It's over, Mac. A few bruises, but we're OK. Our boat didn't sink. Let's just put it behind us," said Mom.

"OK," said Mac, "but it's not the first time in my life that I've demonstrated a total lack of good judgment. Taking risks without evaluating the rewards; that's a problem I can't seem to outgrow."

"Well, I guess I can remember when you and Doc might have drunk one or two more obble gobbles than you needed," said Mom, trying to lighten things up.

But Mac persisted, "I took risks flying fighters when the targets were clearly not worth it. It could have cost the life of a wingman. Yesterday, it could have cost the lives of my family. Just bad judgment, that's all there is to it."

"Let's not go any further with that, Mac. The heat of the battle was a different matter," interrupted Mom.

"Not really. Bad judgment is bad judgment. I'm ashamed and I am truly sorry. It will never, ever happen again – I promise both of you."

I really wanted to get up and give Mac a big hug but, being a dumb bunny, I just sat there and spooned up some eggs. It took Mom to put an arm around both of our necks and pull us into a big family hug.

When the urge to thank God came over me again, I didn't say anything. Not because I thought it might start a philosophical discussion at an inappropriate time, but more because I wanted to do some work on my own beliefs first. Right then I was sort of stuck at stage one: if God saved me, why did he turn my Mexican dancing partner into shark food?

With those thoughts, I went on deck to inspect the morning. We were anchored in Bahia Santa Maria, and a pea-soup fog had engulfed us – perfect conditions for thinking about religion. So I sat down on the forward hatch and stared into nothingness.

When I was in the water, I was sure my life was soon to end. Why did I instinctively turn to God for help? In the cold light of day, Mac's theory that "God's too busy tending to the problems of the universe" made sense to me. Sometimes, though, I found my conversations with Mac quite perplexing, particularly when we got into complicated things like the speed of light and stars that are millions of light-years away. Then there was infinity. Looking into nothing but dense fog, I could think of no better time to ponder that concept. Mac said it would do no good because it was impossible for anyone to envision infinity. He said I should close my eyes and concentrate as hard as I could. Eventually I would see a dark wall, or maybe it would be a white wall, but I wouldn't be able to see or think of a boundless condition.

He said to imagine jumping from the earth, traveling through space, and passing from our solar system into a universe of stars. If I kept flying straight, I would pass more stars, and more solar systems, then still more. I would fly forever, for there was no end to infinity. Mac said that if I could see into the limits of infinity, I would see God. He said that God wouldn't look like a man or a woman; He would resemble a power of energy so brilliant that no words could adequately describe Him. Yet, simultaneously, He could resemble a butterfly or a flower, for He was the essence of nature: nature as we know it on earth, nature of the universe and nature of infinity. That was why He was much too busy to be involved with the everyday problems of individuals.

It all made sense yet, for the first time in my life when I felt that all the chips were down, I prayed to God for help. The fact was that if I ever had to face a life-threatening problem again, I would do the same thing. So maybe it was a matter of degree. If I prayed for help to pass my math exam – well, I should have studied harder instead. Big things might be different. When in a real fix, what else was there to do but scream for help? It didn't seem to help my Mexican ballet partner much but, still, it was a lot better than nothing.

Mom, on the other hand, was a lot easier to understand. She believed that man had used religion for his own benefit. She believed that people have plundered and purged one another, conscience-free, in the name of God since the beginning of time. No religion had believers that were exempt from twisting the word of God to suit their own needs; hating and killing have been condoned forever. Surely, God, if there ever was one, gave up long ago on planet Earth.

Mom said that if Christ were to return to earth, he would join the gay rights movement. Certainly He would condemn those that cloak themselves in Christianity, without ever practicing the basic rules like do unto others.

Like everything else my mom expressed, it came out clear, straight to the point, and usually nothing vague like light-years and infinity. She just had a very skeptical view of religion. Not religions themselves, but the manner in which people manipulate religious teachings for their own benefit.

Maggie, my fabulous stepsister, was a breath of fresh air on any subject. She said her prayers every night and truly believed that God was listening.

But Maggie was perfect – just the opposite from me, a leading candidate for the top ten on God's shit list. Between Maggie, Mom and Mac, I was surrounded by more religious philosophy than I could handle, especially since, without being overly self-critical, I viewed myself, at best, as a self-indulgent, underachieving teenager. I knew it was near time for me to figure out who I was and what I stood for, but that wasn't going to happen right then. I needed to figure out some basics before I could build any meaningful philosophy. Besides, the brief amount of thinking that I had already done had made my brain ache. Pondering religion had to wait. God had been out there for a long time, and any conclusions I might have drawn were not going to make or break His day.

It just occurred to me that I didn't explain how we managed to enter Bahia Santa Maria during the dark of the night. I had been out cold, but Mom told me what I missed. I think it might be worth repeating, for it gives an idea of how we navigate.

As I have said before, Mac was a great seaman. Maybe a little retarded when it comes to retrieving skiffs, but he was a sailor and a superb navigator. We didn't have any fancy electronics, like Loran or even radar. We navigated by dead reckoning, or by keeping track of time, distance, compass headings, and allowing for drift. We plotted an estimated position every hour and confirmed it with an occasional land sighting or sexton reading.

Sailing into Bahia Santa Maria was a classic example of dead reckoning. Mac had to locate a harbor entrance that was totally obscured by darkness and shore fog. When I checked Mac's chart, sure enough, I saw that he had recorded the time when we were abeam of Lazaro Light. From that point, he had drawn a line indicating our course and noted 123 degrees for thirty-nine minutes. He had estimated our speed at seven knots, so in that time, we would have traveled 4.5 nautical miles. Then he made a 90-degree turn to a compass heading of 33 degrees and hoped the entrance was dead ahead. Mom had been on the fathometer calling out the water depth. This was the moment of truth, for as they sailed into the fog bank, they lost all forward visibility. If they had miscalculated, the Sumac might have crashed onto a rocky shoal. There was no Coast Guard to call; they were six hundred miles away. So, when the water calmed and a faint odor of land scented the air, Mac and Mom must have breathed a sigh of relief to know that they were safely inside the harbor. I missed it all, but just looking at Mac's chart made it easy to visualize. We had sailed ahead for a few more minutes, then made another 90-degree turn to the left and powered up into the northwest corner of Bahia Santa Maria, a perfect anchorage.

Noon came quickly and the fog gave way to a bright sunny day. Our brief siesta after the previous day's ordeal was over. Mac, suited up in a mask and snorkel, began an underwater inspection of the Sumac's hull. Dive after dive, he moved from the bow to the stern and found no serious damage. There were no cracked ribs or planks, just a few minor dings and some paint scrapes. The wound on my face kept me sidelined, so I followed along from inside, inspecting all accessible areas of the hull. That there wasn't the slightest indication of a leak spoke well for the soundness of the Sumac's double-planked mahogany hull – a credit to Kettenburg Boat Yard, master builders of wooden boats.

After another day of resting and drying out, we were ready for our trip's final leg to Cabo San Lucas. A 06:00 departure began with an easy sail in mild breezes. Conditions would have been perfect to retrieve a skiff lost at sea but, fortunately, no such challenge confronted us. We simply enjoyed one of those fabulous sailing days when there was little more to do than absorb the idyllic good fortune of being where we were. Time was unaccountable, and soon it was sunset. One more night at sea and we would see the land's end of the Baja California peninsula.

That night's sunset was remarkable. Almost every sunset at sea is an awesome display of red and orange hues which give way to various shades of purple, but this was a special night. Patchy clouds were perfectly spaced to carry a crescendo of colors completely across the sky, all the way to the eastern horizon.

We watched the sunset silently. I don't remember if I was inspired to again think about religion, or infinity, or just what – but I broke the tranquility of the moment.

"Mac, I've been thinking about infinity, and well... How far could really smart people, maybe like Einstein, see toward infinity?"

Mac smiled (he loved this kind of discussion), "Well, Andy, there's no real way to answer. Now Einstein and a lot of smart guys before him could fill a blackboard with numbers explaining infinity, but the fact is they couldn't see or think their way to infinity any better than you or me."

"Come on, Mac. Are you saying that Einstein had no better grasp than I do?"

"Bottom line is yes," said Mac. "No one can see into infinity any more than you, and for one simple reason: there is no percentage of a part of something that is infinite. There is no halfway to forever."

"So that's why you believe in God, Mac?"

"We're getting pretty deep, Andy, but yes. I believe that infinity is why there has been and always will be a God. As long as there are things we do not understand (and that will be forever), the belief in God will prevail."

"Let's talk about something more comprehensible, like life on other planets. You always said that UFOs are for real, so where do they come from?" I asked.

"Well, Andy, I don't see any reason not to believe that there is intelligence on other planets, possibly in undiscovered universes. If that is true, then intelligence should eventually work towards itself. We on Earth will always be probing the universe, and maybe an even more advanced intelligence is probing in our direction. It is inevitable that some form of communication will develop as time goes by."

"That's a perplexing thought, but assuming that intelligence discovers other intelligences, what does that do for us as far as our theory of God? I mean will God diminish in the eyes of future mankind?"

"My guess is that it will be just the opposite. As man becomes more intelligent, and perhaps more aware of other universes, he will also realize more clearly that complexities, like infinity, are and always will be beyond his comprehension. The power of God will actually intensify and become more essential and dominant in the lives of advanced intellectual beings."

Before I could absorb Mac's comments, Mom

spoke up from the galley saying, "I hate to interrupt two great religious philosophers drifting through outer space, but dinner is ready and I need one of you jerks to bring it up to the cockpit."

As we settled down to fried dorado with onion and tomato sauce, Mom said, "Now where were you guys, let's see... finding God on his throne in outer space or... Let's change the subject, for crying in the beer, to something you might have a speck of knowledge about. What's the name of that star you always like to find before you fall asleep, Andy – you know, the one off the lip of the Big Dipper?"

"You mean off the handle of the dipper – that would be Arcturus, Mom."

"And why does this particular star fascinate you," asked Mom.

"Well, because it's bright and easy to find. It is only thirty-seven light-years away from earth, so you were about three years old when the light we see tonight left the surface of the star."

"I happen to be forty-one," said Mom. "Maybe we should move onto another subject, like who's going to take the first watch and who's going below for a rest – but not before you all clean up the galley."

"I could use a nap. Besides, it's a good night for Andy to teach you something about the stars," said Mac as he grabbed our dishes and started below.

Uh oh, I could smell it coming. Mac never hung around for lectures that involved Maggie and me. I guess maybe he remembered when he was young and suffered from hormone-itis. But still, it was his daughter who ran around naked in my mind all day. I was sure he knew it. He was just a super guy for not killing me.

Chapter Nine

The early watch always seems longer, especially when nothing much is going on. A reaching breeze was pushing us along at about six knots, and the sea was fairly flat. Holding the compass course was getting easier as I learned to listen to the sounds of the water and watch the fullness of the mainsail. At first, I just stared at the compass and chased the needle back and forth across the designated heading, but by now even the faintest stars on the forward horizon kept me oriented with an occasional cross-check of the compass.

Oddly, we had sailed for quite a while with hardly a word being spoken. I just steered the boat along, knowing that when Mom was through mulling over her thoughts, the silence would be broken and the first question would not be about stars in the sky.

Eventually, as I predicted, Mom asked, "I really think it's great that you and Maggie are so close, but don't you think it's time that you both broaden your horizons a bit?"

I guess you know by now that Mom rarely beat around the bush. When she had something to say, she pretty much dove right into the guts of things. That night was no exception.

"I thought keeping Maggie in Oregon and me in Baja was designed along those lines," I answered rather curtly.

"That depends on you and Maggie and how fair you are with each other."

We were no longer skidding around the periphery of the issue, so I decided it was time to unleash a hypothetical scenario that I had conjured up just for the occasion.

"Wait a minute, Mom. We know we have a lot of growing up to do, but look at it a different way – what if you and Mac were neighbors, just good friends. Maggie would be living with Mac and I would be living with you. So then I start dating Maggie. See any problems so far?"

"Of course not, but that's not the way it is," answered Mom.

"Seems to me you're letting antiquated social rules run our lives. Mac has always said that society is a bunch of bullshit. Besides, how could it be a sin to love your stepsister? I'll bet there are no laws, social or otherwise, that say loving your stepsister is wrong. I'll bet the Mormons wouldn't give it a second thought," I said with mounting confidence.

"Watch your heading," interrupted Mom, "you're zigzagging all over the ocean. My point is not about social rules, it's about you and Maggie. You both say you love adventure, yet you won't venture beyond your own backyard when it comes to learning and experiencing life and love."

"That's the way it looks, Mom, but that just puts us back to square one. Maggie is off to college and I'm off to Baja. She's probably at a fraternity party with the captain of the soccer team right now. Maybe she will bring him to Mexico for spring break so I can kill him and spend the rest of my life in the Mulege prison."

"Don't be stupid, Andy," said Mom.

"Well, OK, so I don't kill him. Maybe I just cut off his right arm so he can't throw anymore touchdown passes."

"How do you know he's right-handed? Besides, I thought you said he was a soccer player," joked Mom.

"Well, that's a point. I guess I should go back to just killing him. Something simple, like maybe I'll help him drown or shoot him in the stomach with a spear gun."

"You are getting weirder by the minute," said Mom, with a smile.

"Well, on the other hand, I could just let him live, and he will eventually marry Maggie, and then you'll realize that the father of your grandchildren is strong as an ox and has the same I.Q. I can add to the picture by bringing home a girlfriend that resembles something Ole Tiger might drag in. Then, in no time at all, your children will give you a few low-quality, rug-rat grandchildren. They'll probably not be much to look at and they'll certainly be quite stupid, but there will be no danger of any impropriety."

We couldn't hold back a laugh. Mom gave me a hug and we both knew that the lecture, like others in the past, had accomplished nothing. We went back to enjoying the tranquility of the evening and to steering a straighter course.

Around midnight, a phenomenon occurred unlike any other we had ever seen. Mom and I had traded off steering and it was about time for Mac to take over the next watch when we saw what appeared to be a white sandy beach dead ahead. Mac ran to the bow to get a better look. He had just checked the chart and our position plotted to be about halfway between Santa Maria and Cabo San Lucas. We were at least twelve miles off the coast and our fathometer showed we were in over ninety fathoms of water. There could not be a sandbar in front of us, so we held our course. Ten scary minutes went by, and suddenly, we sailed into a phosphorescent sea that produced so much light that it had turned a dark night into day. Sardine-like fish on the surface were so thick that the water looked like a bright cloud. Each fish was feeding on something smaller. Their frantic activity made the water boil, and because of the phosphorescence, it was like watching a giant underwater fireworks display!

The little fish made lights like millions of sparklers while the big fish made tracks like huge skyrockets. The seawater that splashed onto our deck illuminated the boat like a mammoth florescent light. Mac scooped up a bucket of water and dumped it on my head. My whole body glowed like a frightening Halloween character. We soaked ropes in the sea and then twirled them over our heads; they glistened like electric lassos. Down below, the seawater in our sinks and toilets lit up the cabin. It lasted for over half an hour, until we abruptly sailed out of the sea of light and into total darkness. We looked back to see "the white sandy beach" slowly disappearing and wondered if we could ever adequately describe such a phenomenon.

Phosphorescent seas are not uncommon off the California and Baja Coasts; even I had seen them before, but nothing like that. Later, when we met Doc and Lizzie in Cabo San Lucas, we gave them an account and, like everything else that occurs in the ocean, Doc had a long-winded technical explanation. He said that bioluminescence in the water would more accurately describe what we had observed. Basically, there are immeasurable quantities of tiny creatures that float around somewhere between plant and animal life. When enough of them get together, they have the capacity of making one hell of a glow on a dark night. He said a lot more than that, but that's all I remember, except for Mom making one of her famous yawns and Lizzie rolling her eyeballs so far up that all you could see were the whites.

    The next morning we were to have our first view of Cabo San Lucas, marking over seven hundred and fifty miles of sailing since leaving San Diego. It would also represent my longest uninterrupted sail ever. It made me think about some of my non-sailing friends at home and the questions they would ask like, "What's there to do?" and "Won't you get bored just sitting all day long in a sailboat with your parents?"
    I couldn't answer those questions very well before, but after a few weeks of cruising, I could hardly believe the fantastic adventures that I had already experienced: the mystery of the Wind Song, the Eppleton Hall, fish frenzies, trying to rescue a skiff and being bitten by a dead man, phosphorescent seas, Gordo, fishing and whales – not to speak of exhilarating sails and gorgeous sunsets.
    Bored? Not really. I got the shit scared out of me a couple times, but I was never bored.
    Sailing into Cabo San Lucas would mark the end of our Pacific voyage, and I was salivating over the thought of a shore dinner. I slept a little, but around 04:00 I woke up and joined Mac at the helm. About an hour later Mom joined us and we watched the sunrise just as the cape came into view.
    There was land's end in all its glory: two towering three-hundred-foot peaks covered with guano. Called Los Frailes (the friars), they marked the beginning of the incomparable Sea of Cortez.
    I thought out loud, "If you were to miss this spectacular landfall and just keep sailing south,

you wouldn't see anything until you hit Antarctica."

"Well, maybe," chortled Mac, "but after a day or two you might get the inclination that you were off course a bit."

The peacefulness of the dawn was suddenly interrupted by the crackling of the single sideband radio. It was an incoming call from Doc; he had great news. They had been sailing non-stop from Scammon's Lagoon and were estimating an afternoon arrival in Cabo. That added extra anticipation to the shore dinner that we were already drooling over. If the innkeeper of the little Hacienda Hotel did not know about obble gobbles, he would be in for a surprise before sunset.

After taking a roll of photos, we rounded the cape and headed up into the beautiful bay of Cabo San Lucas, then found anchorage off the beach in front of the Hacienda. Mac made a quick trip to the galley and reappeared with a bottle of champagne that he had hidden behind the veggies. Lots of hugs and cheers ensued as we told each other what great sailors we were.

"Here's to Andy – the first kid in history to be bitten by a dead man while being towed behind a sailboat through shark-infested water," toasted Mac.

"Not funny," I said as I gave Mac a shove that flipped him over the rail and into the water.

"Hey, Mac, are you still looking for that stupid skiff? You forgot to put on your swimming shorts," I said just as Mom rammed me from behind and sent me ass-over-teakettle into the water with Mac.

"Last one to the beach is a booby," shouted Mom as she dove off the stern and started swimming toward the shore.

She won but I was a close second, while Mac, who had the swimming style of a wounded Saint Bernard, was a distant last. Just off the shore break we noticed a pipe sticking out of the sand with a short hose attached. Mac said that it was springwater for replenishing boats' water supply. Later that morning we moved the Sumac near the beach and swam a hose ashore. Soon we were filling our water tanks with cool, fresh water.

About lunchtime Mac shouted for Mom to come on deck.

"Look over there toward the old cannery, isn't that the Haileys' boat?" asked Mac.

Mom squinted and said, "Sure looks like a Cal-40. Let's go over and see."

Pat and Sophie Hailey were sailing friends from the San Diego Yacht Club. In fact, their boat shared the same dock as the Sumac and the Sirius. When Pat spotted us rowing over, he did the typical Pat Hailey thing: he pulled out his coronet and cut loose with "When the Saints Go Marching In." Pat was a fabulous horn player, sort of a modern day Muggsy Spanier or Bix Beiderbecke. He could really play Dixieland jazz. His music poured out of his sailboat at all hours of the day and night, sometimes to the chagrin of the early to bedders, but there were always enough aficionados to offset any complaints. It took no urging at all to get an "Absolutely!" from them when Mac asked if they would join us for dinner at the Hacienda.

"We've been cruising around Baja by ourselves for over a month. A party with you guys would be a perfect finale before we bite the bullet and start beating our way north," replied Pat.

Chapter Ten

Around mid-afternoon I spotted a ketch rounding the cape that had to be the Sirius. Minutes later, we were shouting greetings to Doc and Lizzie. It was so good to see them. It seemed to me like a year had gone by since I had visited them in Scammon's Lagoon.

That evening, Mom and Mac rowed the Zodiac over to pick up Doc and Lizzie and I rowed our little fiberglass dinghy ashore. There was a twilight breeze that was freshening, instead of dropping to the customary night calm. We were all too busy with our reunion to notice another ominous sign – the wind had swung around to the south, signifying a weather change.

But we had left our problems behind and the partying spirit escalated dramatically when Mac rowed the Zodiac close to the beach and gave Lizzie the command to jump. She obediently did so, not knowing that the water dropped off steeply only a few feet from the beach. Instead of landing barefoot on the sand, Lizzie was waist-deep in ocean water. All her preparations for a shore party, including her pretty red dress, were totally messed up. Boy, did she let Mac have it! Her Marine vocabulary needed no booze to give Mac the expletives he deserved.

Amidst shouts of "You son of a bitch" and gales of laughter, Mom and Mac jumped out of their dinghy, a lot more gracefully than Lizzie.

The bar and restaurant of the Hacienda was only a few feet up the beach. About ten tables of visiting yachtsmen and hotel guests had launched a sunset happy hour, and margaritas served in glass fishbowls were the order of the day. Without debating over teaching the bartender how to make obble gobbles, our group joined right in with margaritas that required two hands to lift. Mac ordered me a beer as a treat for the special occasion.

Mom offered the first of about fifty toasts. "Here's to a great trip down the coast. Good-bye, Pacific Ocean, and hello, Sea of Cortez!"

As if it were perfectly timed, the beach door to the restaurant burst open and in rolled Pat and Sophie to the tune of "When the Saints Go Marching In."

Everyone in the place rose to form a conga line, and a Cabo San Lucas fandango was underway.

Someone made the mistake of asking Doc about the origin of the Sea of Cortez, and Doc began, "Well, about ten million years ago, an earthquake tore a long chunk off the coast of Mexico that eventually produced the peninsula of Baja. Then, up charged the Pacific Ocean, all the way to the confluence of the Colorado River, forming a great saltwater aquarium. In fact, over seven hundred different species of fish exist here, plus thousands of species of invertebrates. Whales, such as gray, finback, humpback, blue and sperm, along with an enormous variety of gamefish, including marlin, sailfish, yellowtail, sierra, dorado, wahoo and sea bass, just to name a few..."

"Don't stop now, Doc, you're on a roll," said Mac.

"We are about to enter the most phenomenal marine sanctuary in the world," continued Doc. "Maybe thirty kinds of sharks – then add billions of scallops, clams, oysters, lobsters, crabs, shrimp and abalone, and..."

"Don't let me butt in, Doc, but speaking of shrimp, I'll have them with garlic for dinner, if a moment to order is allowed," interrupted Lizzie.

Before any ordering could take place, I made the mistake of asking Doc to give us the reason for the phenomenon.

Lizzie groaned, but undaunted, Doc answered, "Two things: for millions of years the Colorado River has dumped minerals that have built up a gigantic deposit that has, and maybe will always, ooze up and support life in unbelievable quantities. These nutrients, aided by sunlight, enable the growth of microscopic marine algae which, with the help of simple little creatures called zooplankton, support the plankton that is the basic food supply for all the creatures that inhabit the sea. Everything from microscopic organisms to the giant baleen whale which devours about eight tons of it per day have plankton as their primary food. All sea animals either eat it directly or eat the animals that do. Then you have the birds dropping immeasurable quantities of guano, fertilizing the water and adding to the growth of algae. The birds and fish form an interdependence, and their food supply..."

"Jesus, Doc, we're a lot more concerned about our own food supply. If you keep babbling, they're going to close the kitchen on us and I'm not about ready to settle for a dish of guano," interrupted Liz as she ordered six more fishbowls of margaritas for the table.

The menus came with the drinks, then the conversation shifted to the Bryces. The Hailey's had heard about the tragedy, but they had been in Mexico at the time, so they needed to be brought up to speed by our two super-sleuths, Doc and Mac.

Mac reiterated his feeling that the couple I had seen deflating a dinghy on the yacht club dock couldn't possibly be connected to the murderers.

"Too big a coincidence, and besides, it takes a

lot of gall to kill two people, blow up their boat, and then cruise right in to the front dock of the victims' yacht club, pack up a dinghy and quietly walk away," said Mac.

"Maybe – maybe not," Doc said with a substantial burp. He had undoubtedly left his Arm & Hammer on the boat and the margaritas were lighting up his esophagus.

"I'm thinking the killers figured that they would blend right in with the evening activities of a busy yacht club," he continued after catching his breath. "Throw in perfect sea conditions and timing that coincides with the time the crime was committed, and... Well, if they weren't the killers, who were they?"

"OK, so there is a remote possibility that those guys were the bad guys, but they're gone – no clues, no nothing," said Mac.

Then Pat Hailey spoke up for the first time, "Why are you connecting two people you saw on the dock with the Bryces' deaths?"

Doc gave an update, and while Mac prepared to counter with more skepticism, Pat asked me what the couple looked like.

When I was finished, Pat turned to Sophie and asked, "Didn't that woman in La Paz have red hair?"

"Definitely," answered Sophie, "red and quite short."

That got our attention in a hurry. Maybe it was Doc, but it could have been all of us, who asked, "What's the story?"

"Three nights ago, this couple, a red-headed woman and kind of an ugly-looking man, rowed out to our boat. I don't know how, but they seemed to know we were leaving for Cabo in the morning. They acted real friendly and asked if they could get a ride back to San Diego. I didn't like the looks of them so I had to think fast," said Pat, "but, before I could answer, Sophie spoke up, saying that we would be happy to take them but we had some logistic problems to work out. A couple guys in my band were planning to travel with us. In fact, we were just on our way ashore to meet them... Looking back, it really scares me to think how fast Sophie can think up an absolute lie and tell it with such a straight face."

"That's easy to understand. The obvious fact is that women are a hell of a lot smarter than men," said Lizzie as she raised her margarita bowl triumphantly.

After Mom and Sophie seconded Lizzie's insight with appropriate glass clicking, Pat continued, "We both had an uneasy feeling that they wanted to be invited aboard, but Sophie's quick thinking seemed to discourage them. So after saying that they would check back with us in the morning, they rowed away. Afterwards, Sophie remarked that maybe we had been a little rude, but the matter didn't enter our minds again – until tonight."

I was stunned. Their descriptions matched the couple that haunted me. Doc jumped all over the story.

"You guys might well be the luckiest, or maybe the smartest, sailors in Baja. That couple might have been making a hit on you," said Doc.

There was a serious pause in conversation. Even Lizzie appeared to be contemplating the possibility.

Then Mac broke the silence with, "Well, what happened next?"

"Not much," said Pat. "As I said, they rowed away and we never saw them again. The next morning, a Mexican dockworker... I can't remember his name, but I think it started with 'W', like Wooly or something. Any rate, he came out to our boat and said that the people that had rowed out the night before had asked him to say thanks for considering taking them north but they had a change in plans."

After another lull in the conversation, Mac, still playing the skeptic, said, "So Andy sees a weird couple on the yacht club dock and, a few weeks later, two people ask for a ride north. Now we have two sightings of the Bryces' killers. Only problem is we have zero evidence. Odds are that they're not the same couple. There are lots of red-headed women with ugly boyfriends roaming all over the place. Look at Sophie. She's got red hair, and Pat's not much to look at."

That remark got a laugh out of Lizzie only, but then, she'd had enough margaritas to laugh at anything.

Doc got us refocused, "I'll tell you something, Mac. Your zero evidence remark is bullshit. Just revisit some facts, starting with John Swingler's photograph of the Wind Song leaving Cabo. It has been reported that the enlargement clearly shows a partially deflated rubber dinghy sprawled on the deckhouse. The Bryces' dinghy was stowed, as is appropriate for cruising, on stern davits so no question about it – that deflated dinghy belonged to intruders. A few hours after the Wind Song blows up, Andy sees two strangers deflating a dinghy on the yacht club dock. Now, weeks later, Pat and Sophie are confronted by similar-looking people rowing around in a rubber dinghy. I think there is a lot of evidence, and it totally baffles me that you are so damn skeptical."

"Come on, Doc, don't get your undies in a bunch," quipped Mac.

"Before you make light of the evidence, there is one serious matter you should consider: if they are the culprits, Andy may be the only living soul that can identify them as suspects," said Doc rather ominously.

"Hey, Andy, good old Doc is setting you up for a humdinger of a nightmare," joked Lizzie.

"Don't mean to," answered Doc. "But, even though it is really remote, we should have a couple of codes worked out, just in case."

"Son of a bitch, Doc, I think the margaritas are getting the best of you. Maybe you ought to swim back to the boat and take a shot of your Arm & Hammer," said Lizzie.

"All I'm saying is a little caution does no harm. But you crazy bastards, you just charge ahead without the slightest regard for any possibility of danger," burped Doc.

"I'm with you, Doc. If your theory is correct, I'm the target. I don't want to ever see those creeps again, much less to have them after me. So what did you have in mind for codes," I said.

"Something simple, like if one of us has a problem we raise the yacht club burgee upside-down, and on the port yardarm, instead of the starboard," suggested Doc.

"Very clever, Doc. If we get invaded by killers, all we have to do is say 'excuse me', go hoist the burgee upside-down, and you'll come streaking across the water from wherever the hell you are and save us in the nick of time," said Mac.

"Maybe you ought to go back to lecturing about the Sea of Cortez," said Lizzie, as everyone but me doubled over laughing.

Doc had some other suggestions, like coughing before you say the name of your boat during a radio transmission, but his audience was definitely not with him.

The fourth round of fish bowls arrived, and our little group was not in a mood to worry about anything, not even the fact that the wind was freshening out of the south. The sounds of the slatted windows vibrating and palm leaves rustling reminded me of a very old movie. I think it was "Key Largo" with Humphrey Bogart or Edward G. Robinson, or maybe both of them. They were gangsters in a room like our dining room, and a hurricane was moving in on them. It was a really scary scene.

Everything on the menu sounded great. There were lots of fish and shrimp dishes, but we had the drools for Mexican food so we all went for the combination plate: two *tacos*, two *enchiladas*, a *chili relleno*, *carne asada*, *frijoles* and rice. I devoured every bit of it!

Then Mac began his rendition of trying to save the skiff. When he got to the part where I was spinning like a pinwheel in the water with the dead Mexican fisherman, I started to feel a little queasy, so I excused myself and said I would row the little fiberglass dinghy back to the boat.

Mac followed me to the beach, apologizing all the way, "I am sorry for being so damn insensitive, Andy."

"No, it's just me, Mac. I'm over it and the retelling of me spinning around in the water is really pretty funny. I'm just a little tired. Don't worry, but watch the wind, it seems to be picking up."

Rowing back against the wind and choppy sea was no easy task. Even though it was only about one hundred and fifty yards to the boat, my dinghy was half full of water by the time I got there. So, instead of letting the dinghy trail behind the stern of the Sumac, I bailed it out, fastened the davit lines and pulled the dinghy from the water.

No sooner had I completed that task, when a pounding sound coming from the bow made me run forward. The building sea was lifting the bow out of the water, which in turn slackened the anchor chain, then when the bow fell back and the chain went taut, it made a crunching clang against the bow roller. After watching the chain pound away on the bow roller for a few minutes, I realized that if the waves kept building, the slamming force of the anchor chain would soon destroy the entire bow.

I was in a total quandary over what to do, when I saw the flicker of a spotlight from shore. I knew it had to be Mac and Mom signaling that they were starting back. In the short time since I had left the beach, the wind had more than doubled to fifty knots and the sea was building accordingly. Mac and Mom were in for a nasty row. I doubted they could make it without swamping, but I figured the worst that could happen was that the wind would blow them directly back onto the beach. Under normal circumstances, a night ashore in the little Hacienda Hotel would be great for them, but that would have left me alone on the boat with the anchor chain pounding a big hole in our bow.

I could see the glimmer of the light that Mom must have been shining as Mac rowed his fool head off. They were hardly making any progress, when it occurred to me to tie a long line to the man overboard pole and let it drift back toward my struggling parents. The strobe light on top of the overboard pole worked like a charm. I let it run back almost its full two-hundred-foot length, then I wrapped the end three times around one of the big headsail winches and prayed that Mac had the strength to make it to the overboard pole. A few minutes went by when all of a sudden the strobe light went off and the line attached to it went taut. I started slowly cranking in the line.

The waves must have been lifting the dinghy's bow out of the water, for periodically, I would get some slack that made it easy to grind in a few feet of line. After about half an hour of cranking with one arm and tailing the line with the other, I was running out of gas. I guessed that the rowing must have been near breaking Mac's back, too.

Then I heard Mom shout, "Cleat the line, Andy. We're right below the transom and I have hold of the railing. I need a pull to get aboard."

In seconds, I had her arm and she was safe in the cockpit. Mac bailed out the rubber dinghy, which by then was totally awash with seawater. Then, Mom and I gave Mac a boost and the three of us were together again, soaking wet but safe.

Mac did not need me to tell him that the anchor chain was about to destroy our bow. He grabbed two of our stoutest docking lines, and lying on his stomach at the very tip of the bow, he tied them to the anchor chain as far ahead of the bow as he could reach. As soon as they were secure, I pulled the two lines taut and guided one through the starboard mooring pad eye and the other through the port pad eye. Then Mac cleated the lines securely and slightly released the brake on the anchor chain windlass, releasing a few feet of chain. The two ropes instead of the chain started to take the shock of the bow heaving out of the water. The ropes created a bridle that acted as a shock absorber, so even though the bow still lifted high in the air with each big wave, the pounding stopped and our anchor roller and bow were no longer in danger.

I have said before that Mac is a master seaman. Just like an old fighter pilot: when it's time for action, he can turn off the effects of a bunch of margaritas and get the job done. Why his bell did not ring earlier before the storm was at full intensity, I do not know.

It seems strange for me, a delinquent teenager, to be questioning Mac's judgment again but that evening even old reliable Doc had his head up and locked. Still, Doc did set double anchors before he went ashore and his anchor lines were rope, (except for about fifty feet of chain at the anchor end), so he had no reason to worry that his bow would be bashed apart. Confident that the Sirius could ride out the storm and that it would be impossible to row against the storm with four people in our dinghy, Doc and Lizzie elected to sleep ashore at the inviting Hacienda.

After the Sumac's bow was safe, Mac decided we should take turns checking that our anchor was secure. Mom said that we could manage nicely without her participation and, receiving no argument from Mac or me, she retreated to her cabin. For the next four hours, we took turns going forward to the bow and running a hand out on the anchor chain. If the anchor was dragging we would feel a vibration, but nothing so threatening developed. By 03:00 the wind began to ease and by sunrise the anchorage was a flat calm.

Such was the nature of a treacherous chubasco. It gave little warning: our barometer had not dropped the slightest when we went ashore to party, but the storm hit with hurricane force. Fortunately, it didn't last long. The damage the storm caused was mostly on land. Some old palm trees went over and a few palapa roofs in the village were blown off, but the boats at anchor all seemed to have survived. Some had snarled up gear and most of the dinghies were awash, but there was no serious damage.

The sand bottom of the bay had proven to be an excellent holding ground, even though it was completely exposed to a blow from the south. Our anchor, a CQR (which is shaped like a big plow), simply dug deeper and deeper as the stress on the chain increased. That the anchor did not give was reassuring, but it also created another problem: how to get the imbedded anchor unstuck from the ocean bottom. Normally, we would have powered the boat slowly forward as the electric anchor windlass cranked in the chain. When the boat is directly over the anchor, its handle rises, tipping its flukes upward thus freeing it from the bottom. But that wasn't the case with us, nor the other boats in the bay, that morning. A variety of ingenuities were on display, including diving to anchors to work them free. This practice was confined to the more exuberant, or perhaps more athletic, sailors. That did not include us.

Mac, naturally, had his own system for the occasion. It required backing the Sumac toward the ocean so the anchor would be pulled in the opposite direction from where it was set, then repeating the same activity toward the shore. Our old GMC 353 diesel engine was doing a lot of barking, but eventually the anchor broke loose and clanged against the bow roller. It was covered with mud, signaling a cleaning job for me.

By the time we reset the anchor, Mom had breakfast ready. To my delight, the main topic of conversation was my quick thinking in sending the overboard pole back to rescue Mom and Mac. Although I didn't say it, I silently agreed that it was a stroke of genius on my part. Stories about me doing something creditable were few and far between, so I hoped that this story would stay in circulation for a while. Maybe the news would even get back to God and have a positive effect on my shit list rating. But then, according to Mac, God was much too busy to be bothered by the activities of any individual. I tended to agree with Mac, for if there was truth to his theory, God would have no shit list and I would have a lot less to worry about.

My wishful daydream snapped when hails from Doc and Lizzie came from beside our stern. A local mechanic by the name of Red Rider, (though he didn't have red hair), had taken them back to their boat to investigate a problem, and they had then rowed over with hopes that breakfast was still available. Naturally, Mom had made sure that it was.

The batteries on the Sirius were all but dead, and Doc had determined that a faulty alternator was causing the problem. It just could not put out enough power to keep the batteries charged. Luckily he had met Red Rider on the beach that morning. He had a used alternator off an old truck that should work just fine. In the meantime, he had lent Doc a portable gasoline generator to recharge the Sirius's batteries.

It seemed as if every boat in the bay was having some sort of problem, and this Red Rider guy was as busy as a spider hopping from one boat to another. He was easy to spot – he wore shorts and beat-up tennis shoes and he carried a small tool kit in one hand. He always, always, always had a beer in the other.

All morning long we heard the generator banging away on the deck of Sirius. After several hours, Red returned with an alternator and we all went over to watch the installation. Much to our chagrin, the generator engine ran but it did not provide a charge. Unfortunately, its coil had burned out because the battery cables were placed on the wrong nodes. One of the basic rules repeated over and over by seamen is "red on positive." Well, Lizzie had done just the opposite. Their main battery was history and Red's generator was in need of major repair.

Doc and Lizzie were mortified, but we all soon learned what a great person this Red Rider was!

"Don't worry," he said, "I'll find a new battery for you. In the meantime, my youngest daughter's birthday party is tonight. You would all do me a great honor if you would come to the party."

Then, he disappeared with the remains of his generator. We just stood in amazement while Lizzie, with substantial help from Doc, admonished herself for her stupidity.

At sunset, we all rowed ashore in our rubber dinghy. Everyone, including Lizzie, managed a dry landing on the beach, and off we went in search of the birthday party.

The dirt streets in the little village of Cabo San Lucas were mostly unmarked, but Red's directions were good and soon we were being ushered into his palapa-roofed house as if we were long-lost family members.

Red was an Englishman who had been determined to escape the formalities of a structured life. Somehow, he had found his way to Cabo San Lucas and became a much-needed marine mechanic. He had married a lovely Mexican woman and was about to celebrate the first birthday of their sixth baby girl.

Not just our host and hostess, but all their local guests, warmly took us in. Before long we actually did feel like family. Everyone was dressed up – even Red had put on a white shirt. Like most Mexican kids, all the children were immaculate and courteous: far surpassing the good manners of any little kids I knew at home. Red gave a long toast in Spanish to his little girl, Sonia. We didn't understand it all but we knew it was mighty sentimental for Red had tears running down his face from the very beginning. Before he was through, we were all in tears.

Then came singing which was followed by dancing. That was when bare-footed Lizzie became the star of the Rider's little patio. There was beer for the adults and fruit punch for the kids, but some of the adults were lacing their drinks with stashed tequila. Lizzie had obviously found the stash, or at least one of her dancing partners had led her to it, for she was hitting on all cylinders.

Finally, long after Sonia had been put to bed, *comida* was served inside the casa. Such Mexican food I have never tasted before or since – especially the tamales. I am quite sure I devoured at least six of them.

Eventually, after many warm good-byes, we wended our way back to the dinghy. Lizzie needed an occasional course correction but beyond that we all glowed with the awesome pleasures of the evening. It was the best celebration that any of us could remember. What good fortune to have been included, and what a contented man was Red Rider.

Chapter Eleven

Dawn came too soon – only fighter pilot Mac was up to greet it. Then he started his damn, "Daylight in the swamps, rise and shine, up and at 'em" routine.

Even Mom thought it was obnoxious and let him have it with, "Pipe down, for crying in the beer!"

It didn't work, though. "Persistent" was one of the adjectives used most often for describing Mac. Soon we were sailing east toward Punta Los Frailes, our evening destination.

By noon, we were anchored off a delightful crescent beach directly in front of the Hotel Palmilla. Owned by the Rodriguez family (as was the Hacienda at Cabo San Lucas), this small hotel radiated the very essence of Mexican charm. White walls sprawling with bougainvillea accentuated gorgeous tile floors. Everything was immaculate, including the beautiful young Mexican maids who scurried about in pastel-colored uniforms so crispy fresh that, surely, they must have been changed every hour.

Because we were wet from swimming to shore, we sat on the outside balcony by the bar. The ocean view below, with the Sumac as its centerpiece, made a dream picture beyond description. Reveling in our good fortune, (a frequent habit), we munched a lunch of shrimp and sipped some ice-cold Bohemia. Our drummer didn't let the moment last long, though. Before our plates were clean, Mac paid the bill and hurried us on our way.

Between the beach and our boat we snorkeled above crystal clear water that covered a reef inhabited by enough species of fish to delight any marine biologist. In the midst of our viewing, we noticed that we were not the only mammals in the water. A herd of cattle that we had seen on the beach was taking a swim – though not voluntarily, for some were tethered to a skiff and the rest were playing follow the leader in the direction of a rusty old freighter. Amazed, we swam back to the beach and watched as, one by one, each cow was hoisted out of the water and dropped onto the freighter's deck. We later learned that they were taking a one-way trip across the Sea of Cortez to Mazatlan.

"Now we know what being shipped to market means," quipped Mac.

"Such humor," said Mom. "Let's race to the boat. Mac, to make it fair, you start now, and when you get halfway, we'll start."

"Very funny," said Mac, as he plunged into the water and started swimming with a style that resembled the cows'.

Mom and I tied, and as we watched Mac struggle, Mom suggested we lower a hoist from the mast and help the old boy aboard.

A lazy afternoon sail brought us to Punta Los Frailes. This is the eastern-most point of Baja and it forms a perfect crescent bay – an excellent anchorage, except in southwest winds. We anchored off a sandy white beach that beckoned us to swim in for a visit. We had the place almost entirely to ourselves. We shared it with a Mexican fisherman who had landed his pango nearby and was throwing a net to catch small fish for bait. He twirled the net over his head, much like a cowboy with a lariat, and it would land on the water in a perfect circle. Then, by pulling on perimeter lines, he would purse the net into a pocket, trapping several small mullet-like fish. He placed the live bait in the bottom of his wooden boat, which had been filled with enough seawater to keep the fish fresh. Next he paddled his log-shaped boat out into the ocean where he would fish through the night for sierra, yellowtail and dorado. Before sunrise he would be landing at his village on the north side of Punta Los Frailes.

Now we were alone in paradise, and the brilliance of another great sunset was in the making. We were again assessing our good fortunes when the static from our single sideband radio got our attention. It was Doc. They were still in Cabo. Red Rider had fixed them up with a new battery and a workable alternator, and Lizzie had used the time to recuperate from her over-indulgence at the birthday party. Early the next day they would leave for Cabo Pulmo. Doc was excited, for besides being the only live coral reef in the Sea of Cortez, it was a collecting spot coveted by marine biologists.

Before signing off, Doc relayed a call from Ron. He reported that more study of John Swingler's photo revealed that objects were tied to the Wind Song's mast.

Doc said, "They resemble jerry jugs, probably for gas. This reinforces the theory that the deflated dinghy was brought on board by the assailants, who used it when they abandoned the Wind Song."

After a pause, Doc went on to say, "It also makes the significance of Andy's observations on the dock more than coincidental, Mac. So maybe it's time you snap out of your skepticism and start to focus on reality."

"Any other ominous news, Doc?" said Mac.

"No, except don't forget the code. SDYC burgee upside-down on the port side," said Doc.

"Now you've done it, Doc. You've blabbed our secret code over the airways and every cut-throat pirate in Baja now knows it! We are doomed for sure," joked Mac.

"Oh shit, you're hopeless," said Doc. "See you in La Paz. This is Sirius – Out."

The next morning we decided to visit Pulma by dinghy since it was only four miles away, and Frailes was a safer anchorage for the Sumac. We dropped the dinghy's anchor just inside Pulma Reef and we started exploring with snorkel gear.

Immediately we were poking each other and pointing, "Look here! Look over there!" It was like we were in a giant aquarium. Everywhere in the shallow water were bright-colored little fish. Some were a cobalt blue, others were bright red or yellow, and some were milky clear and almost transparent. Providing a backdrop for this carnival of colorful fish was a variety of starfish, sea-urchins, anemones, sea fans, oysters, limpets and hundreds of other living things that kept us up late with our identification books.

Diving into the deeper water, we came face to face with a huge variety of big fish, like groupers, tuna and even sharks. Just before we left, I speared a small grouper for dinner.

After hours of intermittent diving and relaxing on the dinghy, it was time to head back to the Sumac. We purred along for a while, then something strange happened – our faithful Seagull stopped. Mac went through the usual checks: it wasn't out of gas, the air intake was open, etc. It just would not start. So we were in for a long row.

This was not a serious problem, though. It might cause a blister or two, but there was little wind or sea to make it really difficult. Mac started rowing, and I began to muse about the significance of Pulma Reef. It was a special place made famous thirty years ago by John Steinbeck in his book, The Log of the Sea of Cortez. I loved that book, especially Steinbeck's description of exploring the reef with his biologist friend, Ed Ricketts.

As I watched our outboard uselessly trailing its propeller behind the dinghy, I thought again of Steinbeck and his description of their insidious little outboard engine. He describes it as lazy and refusing to run except for times when rowing would be a pleasure. 'Maybe that's a trait found in all outboards,' I thought to myself as I watched Mac huffing and puffing.

"How about some relief," I asked, and instantly Mac turned the oars over to me.

An hour and a half later we were back on the Sumac, sporting a few blisters but famished and ready for a fresh grouper dinner.

Remarkably, minutes before dinner was ready, what should sail into our view but good ole Sirius with Lizzie hanging onto the bow stay and yelling, "Is dinner ready?"

Mom had already calculated the possibility of such an event and had made adequate preparations.

Mac said, "Let's hoist our burgee upside-down and see how Doc reacts to the signal of immanent danger."

"That's a bit like crying wolf," said Mom.

"Maybe, but more important, Doc might power over here with all guns blazing and ruin the tranquility of the evening," chortled Mac.

The First Life of Andy McCurdy

It turned out that Doc and Lizzie were as hungry as we were, so we wasted no time inhaling Mom's culinary magic. Afterwards we got our charts out and talked about places we wanted to see. Doc wanted to spend a couple days exploring and collecting specimens in Pulma, and our plan was to gunk hole our way to La Paz. Top on our list was visiting Isla Espiritu Santo, a gorgeous island about fifteen miles north of La Paz, but we were running low on supplies so La Paz would have to come first.

"Speaking of Espiritu Santo," said Mac, "did we ever tell you about our first visit there?"

"Probably," yawned Doc, "but we've got nothing else to do, so tell us again."

Undaunted, Mac began, "Several years ago, before we had sailboats, Sue and I flew to La Paz."

"God, it was a tiny airplane, like a four-seater, and I was pregnant with Joey and had no place to pee. I thought I was going to die," interrupted Mom.

"Our hotel, the Los Arcos, made up a lunch for us so, with food in hand, we walked to the municipal pier and found an idle fisherman with a skiff who was willing to take us to Espiritu Santo. When we hit the open water Sue asked our guide if there were any whales in these waters and he replied, *'No hay ballena'* – no whales. Before we had time to completely digest this bit of information – less than fifty yards in front of us – emerged a giant finback whale. It breached a couple of times and then disappeared," continued Mac.

"I can still see the expression on our guide's face, his mouth hung open and he looked at me as if I was some sort of *bruja*," said Mom.

Doc ended a short discussion about finbacks in the Sea of Cortez by stating, "No question about finbacks being here. In fact a herd of over one hundred live mainly in the Midriff area about three hundred miles north of here. And, yes, being the second largest animal on earth, they are giants."

I raised my hand, but before I could get my question out, Doc continued, "Before you all ask – the blue whale is the largest, but the finbacks will run eighty-feet long and over seventy-five tons. They are extremely agile swimmers and can cruise at about twenty knots. That's why you saw one down in the southern waters."

"Jesus, Doc, how to fuck up a good story with a bunch of boring facts," interjected Lizzie.

Doc burped with a disclaiming look on his face as Mac went on with the story, saying that after seeing the whale, they traveled all the way to the nearest bay on the southwest end of Espiritu Santo in silence. Finally Mom ventured forward with another question. She asked if there were any black jackrabbits on the island. Apparently, she had read that a strange reverse mutation of rabbits had occurred. Their guide's reply was an emphatic, *"No, absolutemente no hay conejo negro!"*

"Well, you can guess the rest. As we pulled the skiff onto the beach, hippity-hoppity, right in front of us came a very big, and very black, jackrabbit," said Mac.

"That did it. Sue and I found a delightfully shady spot for lunch, but our poor perplexed boatman refused to leave his skiff. I'm sure he felt that the devil was mocking him and that the only thing he longed for was a safe return to La Paz.

"When we finally got back to La Paz, he could hardly wait to tie his boat before running to a group of his *compadres*, and with much gesturing, he told them of his mystifying afternoon. We could not overhear the entire conversation, but as he glanced back at us, we could hear a few words like *bruja* and *diablo* more than once."

Early the next morning we raised our sails from anchor and quietly slipped away, leaving Doc and Lizzie to enjoy a little extra peaceful slumber. For the next three days, we lazily made our way up the east coast of Baja, exploring delightful little gunk holes. Skin-diving captivated us and our spearfishing skills improved dramatically. I discovered that I could hold my breath underwater impressively, allowing time to inspect deep holes. Once I surfaced to report that I had spotted a giant langouste with only one antennae pointing out of its hole.

Mac said, "If its other antennae is aimed back in the hole, it means something else, like a moray eel, is in there. It's bothering him so he's keeping an eye on it."

I dove again and probed the hole with a long Hawaiian sling, causing the lobster to scurry out. From just behind it, a four-foot eel struck at my spearhead. In self-defense, I shot the spear through its mouth and swam for the surface. Mac, noticing the commotion, reached down, grabbed the spear out of my hand, and flipped the eel into the cockpit. This was a mistake because the eel was far from dead. Its powerful body managed to wiggle free of the spear and it was attacking everything in sight. Mac was doing a rather clumsy version of the Highland fling, trying to keep his ankles out of the eel's crushing jaws as he swatted at its head with his trusty fish bat. The gaff hook at the end of the bat speared the eel several times, but that only seemed to increase its rage. I had climbed out of the water and joined Mom on the cabin-top for a front row view of the fight. The winner was undecided and it was clear that Mac could use some help, yet only a fool would have jumped into that small cockpit. The snapping jaws of the eel usually would be enough to paralyze you with fear, but with Mac's windmill flailing of that sharp-hooked bat, there was danger enough to keep Mom and me on the sidelines.

We were definitely on Mac's side and cheered him on enthusiastically, but Mac was tiring. About the time we felt reinforcements might be necessary, he landed a lucky hit square on the eel's head. The blow would have killed an elephant, but it merely dazed the eel. Mac sensed that he had the monster on the ropes, so he pummeled the eel's head until Mom finally jumped into the cockpit and raised Mac's arm, calling the fight a TKO.

I learned quite a bit from that encounter. Don't ever spear an eel. If you mistakenly do so, don't ever bring it aboard your boat. But, if you make that mistake, too, carry a sledgehammer and a chainsaw to defend yourself against the meanest, nastiest, toughest animal in the sea!

After the fight was over, Mac thanked us for the enthusiastic support and said that he might do as much for us if we were ever attacked by a killer sea-serpent.

We laughed, and Mom said, "There will definitely be no plans made for a rematch."

I dove back to the same hole. The lobster had already established single occupancy, for both antennas were pointed forward. It was an easy shot and when I surfaced this time there was celebration. A magnificent dinner was ensured.

We anchored before sunset in a snug little nook called Ensenada de los Muertos. (Mac thought the name was rather fitting after his battle to the death.) Like Frailes, this was a gorgeous crescent bay with a beach guaranteed to be a sheller's paradise. Mom quickly filled her bag with treasures that included a totally-intact paper nautilus. Darkness fell and we were alone to revel once more in private tranquility.

The next day we needed to be in La Paz for two good reasons: Annie and Joey were flying in, and we were running very low on basic supplies. La Paz Harbor was known to be unfit for swimming, so we opted to spend the night in a delightful bay just north of La Paz, called Pichilinque. We anchored off a bank of mangrove brush and fell into the water for a refreshing swim. We soon realized that we had neighbors – hundreds of them – in the form of frigate birds. From a distance we had admired their graceful soaring and their ability to pluck fish out of the water while still in flight. Now we were given an opportunity to view them at close range. Many of the males had large, red bumps in their necks about where an Adam's apple would be. They seemed quite proud of their ability to inflate this balloon-like mass, and we finally determined that this was part of their mating ritual.

A few predictable comments followed, like "a strange place to get an erection." Mac and I thought our comments were hilarious but Mom, as usual, thought our humor was tasteless.

A radio call from Doc and Lizzie interrupted our sunset watch. Lizzie did most of the talking, saying that Doc had spent the last three days cluttering up the boat with a bunch of slimy objects that he had scraped off the bottom of Pulma Reef. She said she was bored and ready for a shore dinner.

Before they signed off, Doc reported that he had checked in with Ron at the club and there were no new clues concerning the murders. However, an alert to all mariners traveling into Mexican waters was recently put out by the Coast Guard. Their feeling was that an attempt to commit another such crime was possible.

Mac signed off saying, "Can't be as big a threat as I had yesterday. Would you believe that a man-eating sea-serpent almost got me? If it hadn't been for my courage and my skillful use of the fish bat, the damn thing would have swallowed me. I might add that Sue and Andy did little but offer moral support from a very safe distance. Never did they lift a finger until long after the monster lay slain."

"What a hero," replied Doc. "Have another drink and we'll see you soon in La Paz. This is Sirius – clear with your station."

Chapter Twelve

Navigating any harbor entrance for the first time requires a good look at the chart. La Paz harbor was no exception, but it was a warm, calm afternoon and we were in a lackadaisical mood. Mac was steering (thank God) and as we passed the first channel marker, he just headed straight for the anchorage about two miles away. All of a sudden, we felt a bump on our keel. Then we felt a series of bumps, and then we came to an abrupt halt. We were solidly aground – stuck in the middle of La Paz Bay where everyone in the world could see us.

Mac gave the engine a couple of blasts in reverse, but all that did was stir up a cloud of sand that could get sucked up into the water intake port, thus causing an even bigger problem.

Mom arrived from below with the harbor chart in hand, saying, "Probably a wee bit too late for this, Skipper."

We did not need the chart to verify what we could already see by looking to our left; clear as day, there were channel markers forming a crescent path from the harbor opening to the anchorage. By now, you probably have guessed that Mac was a man who advocated professionalism, be it on land, sea, or in the air. So when I say that he was mortified, I am making a gross understatement. At that moment, we knew jokes were inappropriate so Mom and I swallowed our smirks and tried to follow an array of orders.

"Andy, get in the rubber dinghy, and, Susan, (I don't recall him ever calling her that before), lower the anchor down to him. Then, Andy, paddle out to the deep water and drop the anchor," ordered Mac as he fought to retain his posture as commander.

We obeyed, and when the anchor hooked the bottom, Mac started the electric windlass and started retrieving chain. When the chain went taut, our bow pinched down, probably getting us more solidly stuck – if that could be possible. Then Mac went below and, for a moment, I thought he was pulling a disappearing act, like the soggy skipper in the "Get Tricksy, get Tricksy" story. But, despite his humiliation, he soon reappeared with a tide table and announced that he had good news and bad news.

"The tide is low, so eventually, we'll be lifted off this damn bar – that's the good news. The bad news is that we have about four hours to wait," reported Mac.

Mom couldn't contain herself and said, "Well, there is more good news. At least Doc and Lizzie won't be sailing in today. Can you imagine the horns and shouts those two would blast at us as they sailed by with their cocktails in hand?" said Mom.

"Yeah, but I dread the stories you guys will make out of this when we all get together again."

Then we all started to laugh and Mac, relaxing a bit, said, "To hell with it, let's have a beer!"

And that is exactly what we did. It's surprising how quickly time passes when you relax and go with the flow. In what seemed like no time, the wind freshened and Mac got the bright idea to raise the sails. The boat heeled over about twenty degrees, breaking our keel out of the sand. Thus, with help from the rising tide, we sailed off the bar and back into the channel. When we got to the anchorage in front of town, Mac selected a spot where we would be off by ourselves. I guess he wasn't ready for boating neighbors to ask what it was like to be stuck on a sandbar.

But Mom, with her usual head-on style, put the issue to bed by saying, "Being stuck on a sandbar for the whole world to see is much like having a big pimple on your face – it bothers the hell out of you, but no one else really gives a damn."

Mac smiled sheepishly and started to reply, but there was nothing to say. We cleaned up a bit, rowed to shore and walked a short distance to the Los Arcos Hotel. From the front veranda we stepped through a big window into the bar. The hotel did have a front door, but no one ever used it to get to the bar.

Mom and Mac ordered margaritas and we organized our shopping list for the next day. At the crack of dawn we each tackled our assignments: water, diesel fuel, ice, groceries, etc. By noon we had the boat loaded and we were off to the airport by cab.

Greeting Joey and Annie was exciting, and I couldn't help noticing their pale indoor appearance that a few days on the boat would straighten out. Even more important, Annie had a packet of mail; and as I expected, there was a letter for me from Maggie on top of the pile.

Dear Andy,

Thanks for the letter you mailed from Cabo San Lucas. I got it a week after you wrote it and it was postmarked L.A. Your friend Red Rider really provides a neat service by sending mail up with returning tourists.

I can't believe that you were knocked overboard and dragged behind the boat as sharks and a dead Mexican tried to eat you! Has Mac completely lost his marbles? What on earth did he have in mind trying to rescue an old skiff in a crashing sea? Thank God you're all right!

School is going OK, except for math. I never could get math in high school and I'm having a worse time in college.

I have dated a couple guys, but none as interesting as you and they are not half as funny. All they want to do is try and make out. Typical juvenile frat boys – drink a lot of beer and run around like idiots. First time away from home, they act like puppies off a leash. A couple years in the army might help them grow up.

So you're still (and always will be) my favorite sweetheart. But, the bad news is that I won't be coming down to Baja for a break. I considered sneaking away early and escorting Annie and Joey, but that didn't feel like the right thing to do.

I thought about making up some excuse around schoolwork, but I have never lied to you and I am not going to start now. I know I promised, but if we are really going to find out about ourselves, it is way too early for us to be together.

Please realize that having separate paths is no more pleasant for me than it is for you. Even though it's torture now, if we just stick with it, we are going to be the winners in the end.

I write this with a tear in my eye and want you to know that no one of any consequence has entered my life. I'm still nuts about you, Andy. Sometimes I wish you weren't my bro, but then there are times when I would not have it any other way. Remember we are very young and we've got time on our side.

Much love, Maggie

A lot of thoughts pounded through my brain. That was not the letter I had hoped for. Why all the philosophizing? So we were young. Why would she blow a chance for us to be together in this paradise? Our motto, carpe diem... What had happened to it?

The cab let us all off at the port captain's office so we could get our papers and crew list re-stamped. I was feeling sorry for myself so I told the gang that I had to run an errand and would meet them back at the boat. The last thing I wanted was my parents getting a drift of my dilemma and starting some sort of sympathy campaign. After all, it wasn't the end of the world; it was just a setback and I needed some time to shake it off.

As I moped along the gravel road that led to the dock in front of Sawyer's Boat Works, I noticed two guys in the boat yard talking to each other. One was Woogie, a drifter sort of guy who picked up change working on boats and doing odd jobs. That morning, he had offered to do some bright work on the Sumac, but Mac had quickly sized him up as a junkie and told him we had no work.

It was the guy that Woogie was talking to who sent a cold chill up my spine. He was too far away to tell for sure, but he bore a frightening resemblance to the yellow-haired, broken-nosed man on the club dock the night of the Bryce murders.

The Sumac was tied to the end of the dock, so I tried to walk nonchalantly down the pier, but my legs felt like they were made of jelly. I don't think the man noticed me though, for his back was partially turned. When I got to our boat I turned to take another look, but he was gone.

I sat down on the dock and my new friend, a Mexican street dog that I had named Ole Yellow, trotted out to greet me. He put his head on my lap and sort of whimpered as if he sensed my worry. As soon as Mac and the family got there I told them the story.

Mac said, "Well, that was a long-distance glance at a guy you might have seen on a dock at night a month ago. Even if it was the same guy, there is no evidence that he committed any crime."

"All I can say is that I've been having nightmares every night and the same scary guy and his scraggy girlfriend are the main characters. The guy I saw with that creepy Woogie was him. I'm sure of it." I wondered what the hell it would take to get Mac's attention.

"Well, Andy, what can we do? Ask the local cop to arrest a man that you think you saw on a dock back in San Diego? Or maybe we should hunt this guy down on our own and beat him to a pulp until he confesses to committing the crime. The only problem with that is we're the ones they'll throw in jail. So let's put this aside and think about it for a while. When we get back, we'll discreetly ask some questions. A couple of the guys at Sawyer's yard are dependable, and if that guy is still around, they can give us information without putting any unwanted light on us. If, by chance, this is the murderer, he might not have a clue that we know anything. Let's not tip our hand."

I knew what Mac had said made sense but I still didn't appreciate his passive attitude. I knew that Doc would have been a hell of a lot more alarmed. But I was feeling sorry for myself because Maggie wasn't coming down; seeing that guy just added to my torment. It was easy for me to let my imagination get out of control, so this guy with Woogie was probably not the same jerk I saw on the dock – then it hit me.

"Hold it, Mac. What was the name of the boatyard worker who rowed out to deliver that message to Pat and Sophie? They said it started with 'W' – like Wooly. Sure as we are sitting here, Mac, that was Woogie."

"You're dreaming up a self-fulfilling prophecy, Andy. Keep working on it and the bad guys will get you for sure," replied Mac.

His indifferent attitude was really getting to me, but before I could answer, Joey screamed, "Hot dog! We hardly get here and already we're in the middle of a Baja murder mystery."

Trying to put an end to it, Mac ordered, "Everybody aboard. We're off to the peace and quiet of Espiritu Santo. We'll put Joey on night watch for the bad guys."

"Great," said Joey. "I'll be ready with my high-powered slingshot and a bunch of steel pellets."

Chapter Thirteen

The island of Espiritu Santo was actually two islands connected by an isthmus. A hand-drawn chart by an old Baja sailor named Conant gave us perfect directions. By taking a bearing off a century plant high on a bluff, we found secure anchorage in a beautiful, all-weather bay. It was like having our own private lake.

All five of us piled into the rubber dinghy, paddled out to some huge rocks that guarded the bay's entrance and fell into the water. As usual, we were greeted by exotic little fish of all colors in the shallow water. Some of them – like the queen angel, the trigger and the clown fish – we could now call by name. On my first dive into deeper water, I spotted a golden grouper. I surfaced to make my announcement and everyone, even Mac, followed me back down. To our delight, it turned out that there were three golden groupers, each peering out of its own private cave. We were tempted to spear one, because they were the perfect size for dinner, but because of their rarity we thought better of it and settled for a *cabrilla*.

Annie and Joey were amazing. They took to snorkeling like old pros. Annie swam right beside me and I'll be damned if she didn't hold her breath just as long as I did.

We spent the next day on the whitest beach in

The First Life of Andy McCurdy

the world. You've heard me rave about other beautiful white beaches in Baja, but the beach of Eclipse Bay took an undisputed first place. Mom never straightened from her bent-over position, and in a few hours she doubled the size of her already abundant shell collection. The rest of us went after butter clams, and after filling three buckets, we discovered a crop of pen scallops in knee-deep water. What treasures! Each shell contained a fist-sized ball of succulent meat.

Lengthening shadows told us when it was time to paddle our harvest back to our snug hole in the isthmus.

So went another two days of enjoying the secluded paradise of perhaps one of the most beautiful islands in the world. We could have stayed in Espiritu Santo forever, but time was flying by. We reluctantly moved north to San Francisco – another postcard island with a crescent bay. Again, we had the whole bay to ourselves. Or at least we thought we did, until a big stinkpot roared in and dropped its anchor on top of us. As if that wasn't bad enough, they fired up a big generator, polluting the bay with noise and exhaust. Two fat slobs were sitting on a gigantic fantail deck drinking cocktails and playing cards. They were impervious to our glares, so up went our anchor and we moved to the opposite end of the anchorage to reestablish some tranquility. Later, I was getting ready to take Annie and Joey reefing when the same guys came charging across the bay in a Boston Whaler and banged up against our dinghy.

"How about coming on over to our boat for a couple drinks," said one of the men.

He had a half-inflated inner-tube belly and a

pock-marked nose that resembled a large Idaho potato. Mac was half-asleep on the cockpit settee and Mom was reading. For a long moment there was no response from either of them.

Finally, Mac partially lifted the magazine from his face and said, "We've made other plans for tonight."

Mom never even looked up. Those guys must have been used to getting the cold shoulder, for they just continued babbling, oblivious that the conversation was only one way. Finally, they followed me and the kids out to a nearby reef and watched us snorkel. When Joey surfaced with a dinner-sized sea bass on the end of his spear, I thought they were going to fall out of their dinghy.

"Holy shit, kid, how'd you do that?"

"Just swam down and shot it. We need it for dinner," said Joey.

"Any more down there like that?" asked Potato Nose.

"Sure, but you can have this one if you want," said Joey.

"Gee, thanks, kid," and they grabbed the sea bass and sped back to their seventy-eight-foot yacht, the Sea Smasher.

We had planned an early morning departure because that was the way Mac did things. It didn't matter if we had a long way to go, or a very short way to go; he loved to leave early in the morning. As we were retrieving our anchor chain, the crackle of our single sideband signaled an incoming call. It was Doc and Lizzie again. They were just leaving La Paz with fresh supplies. A rendezvous was planned at a mainland cove called Agua Verde.

Of all the little hideaways we found in the Sea of Cortez, this was maybe our favorite. A mountain rose straight up from the sea and split the picturesque bay into two coves. A tiny village was nestled into the south cove, so we anchored in the unoccupied cove to the north. We were protected to the east by a jagged point that gave way to a long underwater reef. An enticing beach was an easy swim away to the north.

Joey and Annie had their snorkels and fins on before the anchor hit bottom. I wasn't quite so eager, but hurried along to join them on a dive to a reef that was deep and open to the sea. The reef might house any species of fish and Joey and Annie's little white bodies could look mighty delectable to an eight-foot hammerhead shark. A couple of dives revealed perfect snorkeling grounds that went all the way to the point. After that, the water quickly deepened and grew murky. I declared that proceeding beyond the point was out of bounds.

As we returned to the boat to give our report, a familiar-looking shrimp boat entered our cove. We could tell by her slight starboard list that it was the Maria. Soon we were greeted by a wave from Jose, her captain. Twice before we had met this jolly band of fishermen and exchanged some commodities. They preferred cans of fruit, and we, of course, craved their fresh camaron. After lots of friendly greetings we agreed to do a shore dinner together on the beach, then they powered over to the village cove. We later learned that many of the crew had wives and family in the little village, so their homecoming, together with our reunion with Doc and Lizzie, spelled the possibility of a real fandango.

Late that afternoon, Jose brought the Maria back to our cove. Fifteen men and women began shuttling to the beach in their one and only little dory. The plan was for them to supply shrimp and red snapper and for Mom to make a ton of pasta and salad. Also, Mac was to bring what he thought would be an adequate supply of *cerveza*.

As we prepared for our trip ashore, the Sirius sailed around the point. Doc and Lizzie recognized the makings of a fiesta. Lizzie's contribution was a half-gallon of rum which quickly made her the most popular person at the party. At first she protected her bounty like a mother tiger, but after a couple of belts, she was showing the boys how to swig the bottle over their shoulders, Kentucky-hillbilly style.

A sumptuous dinner was followed by hours of singing and general frivolity. It was truly an evening that would never be forgotten. When the party ended, we paddled our way back to our respective boats and Captain Jose slowly powered his happy crew back to their village cove.

Just when it seemed that a bit of silence might enhance the beauty of our anchorage, a bellowing noise started from the beach. It resembled the moaning and groaning of a lovesick hyena, and it lasted the rest of the evening. We surmised that some poor man had taken a bit too heartily to rum drinking (Kentucky style) and had been left by his mates to sober up on the beach. We criticized Lizzie the next morning; if she had allowed him a swig or two more, he might well have passed out on the beach and we'd have all gotten a quieter night's sleep.

In the not-so-early morning, we parted company with Doc and Lizzie again. They stayed on for some local exploring and we headed back south to search for a gunk hole that Mac and Mom were curious about. It was a small, shark-fishermen's village called Puerto Gato, and it was protected by a series of shallow reefs. The waters were very tricky to navigate but with the help of Conant's hand-drawn charts, we were able to weave our way through and drop anchor right off the beach.

Shark fishermen are nomadic. They have special camps ashore where they dry their catch on large indentations in rock. From the remains of old fires and the stench of decaying shark carcasses, we knew that they had vacated camp not too long ago.

The sentinel reefs were perfect for shallow snorkeling, and because of the shark debris, the bird life was incredible – especially the pelicans. Obviously accustomed to people, the pelicans quickly became our pets. Annie speared a little fish and soon a pelican was sitting next to her enjoying a snack. Joey took a lazier approach, with a bunch of over-the-hill tortillas he hand-fed a small squadron.

The sun's reflection on the water hampered our visibility as we tried to navigate the submerged reefs that guarded Puerto Gato. Just as we thought we had made it to open water, our prop hit something very solid. It must have been a spear of coral rock sticking out from the side of the reef. It did not strike our keel, but when the coral hit our propeller it made a real clunk. When we dove to make an inspection we saw no visual damage to the shaft, but the prop had a nasty gash in one of its blades.

The damage was sufficient to create a noticeable vibration when Mac revved up the engine. So, we limped back to La Paz knowing that a couple days for repairs were in order.

Chapter Fourteen

After it was removed by a diver at Sawyer's Marine, we saw that the propeller was banged up more than we had thought. For the next two days a mechanic hammered on the dents and then refitted the prop to the shaft, but the vibration was still there. The motor was safe to operate at low rpms, but after a period of time, damage to the shaft and stuffing box could occur. Over our radio telephone, Mac discussed the problem with friends at Kettenburg Marine back in San Diego. They agreed to rustle up a new prop and find a way to ship it to La Paz.

All of this had put Mac in a mood that was totally at odds with the glorious sunrise that announced another perfect day in Baja. Then, from out of nowhere, the two goons from the stink pot, the Sea Smasher, powered along our side in their sporty Boston Whaler.

I had guessed Mac would brush those turkeys off faster than he did in Isla San Francisco, so I was amazed when he said, "What's up, boys. What do you need?"

"Well, we were wondering if you and your boys would show us how to do that spear-fishing," said the one with a nose like an Idaho potato.

I chuckled to myself thinking how quickly Mac would shut off their water, when he answered,

"What exactly did you guys have in mind?"

"Well, if you would come with us on our yacht, we could be back to that island in about two hours and then take it from there. We'll pay you three hundred dollars for your efforts," said Potato Nose.

My jaw dropped to the deck when Mac answered, "Sounds like a deal. We'll come over to your boat in about an hour."

As they pulled away, Mom yelled up from the galley, "I can't believe it! You're going skin-diving with those two rum dumbs. You've lost your mind, Mac."

"I think it sounds like fun," said Annie.

"I want to go, too," piped in Joey.

"No way," said Mom. "It'll be a cold day in hell before I let you kids go onto that floating den of iniquity."

"Three hundred bucks will pay for a new propeller," said Mac.

"You'd do anything for money, and so would you, Andy," blurted Mom.

"Jeez, I haven't said a word and I'm already in trouble," I whined.

"Well, I'm not letting Mac go alone, so you can tag along – but, just for once, stay out of trouble," pleaded Mom.

From the flying bridge the captain of the Sea Smasher welcomed us aboard.

"Where do you fellows recommend – Espiritu Santo or San Francisco?"

"What's your cruising speed?" inquired Mac.

"Pending on sea conditions, an easy fifteen to twenty knots," replied the captain.

"Better chance for big fish at San Francisco," said Mac.

"OK, we'll be anchoring inside the cove in about

two hours. Have a look around and come up on the bridge when you feel like it," said the captain.

The cockpit of the Sea Smasher flaunted a luxurious setup for deep-sea fishing. There were four fighting chairs that looked like therapeutically designed dentist chairs; they revolved and tilted electronically, and could move on a track to comfortably face a table specifically designed for card playing and drinking. This was undoubtedly the place where Potato Nose and his companion, who we had nicknamed Pumpkin Head (because of the size and color of his head), logged their most constructive time.

They were both in the main saloon. Potato sat behind the saloon's four-stool bar in an elevated, mahogany skipper's chair. Pumpkin squatted in one of the stools. Their 08:00 Bloody Marys were all but history, so our arrival warranted a refill. They offered one to us too, but Mac declined for both of us, accepting a beer for himself instead.

"Well, Mac, think we'll see some big ones today?" asked Pumpkin Head.

"Probably – but it will take a couple hours to get there, and gin and diving don't mix too well," said Mac in a tone that might have impressed a group of Sea Scouts, but not those two reprobates.

"Don't worry, boys. Deede and me, we never mix our diving with too much drinking," said Pumpkin Head.

"That's right," said Potato Nose. "Once our face masks are on, it's strictly business for us, and bad news for the giant groupers."

"Mind if we look around?" asked Mac.

"Be my guest, *mi barco es su barco*," said Potato, probably using the only Spanish words he knew.

The First Life of Andy McCurdy

From the saloon, we walked up two steps to a pilothouse that featured the best in electronic gear: Decca radar and auto pilot, Loran, high-seas single sideband radio, VHF and low-frequency AM radios, three depth sounders, and a skipper's chair with shoulder straps and foot stirrups that resembled the seat of a jet fighter. The chair was mounted on a track so that it could move to either starboard or port, thus the skipper could handle all the equipment without moving from his seat.

Two steps led down to a great cabin for guests and forward to two forepeak cabins for crew. The owner's cabin was aft under the main cockpit, and the engine room was under the pilothouse.

On both sides of the pilothouse were doors that gave access to ladders to the flying bridge. We climbed up to meet Captain Doug Blackburn, a friendly sort who appeared to know his business.

"Do you fellows have local knowledge of the waters around the anchorage?" asked Captain Doug.

"Sure," said Mac, unfolding Xerox copies of Conant's hand-drawn charts.

The captain was duly impressed. He requested a set for himself when he learned that they covered about forty uncharted anchorages in the Sea of Cortez.

After a brief exchange, we learned that Doug had been the skipper of the Sea Smasher since her launching in Miami five years ago, and he had sailed her around to Marina del Rey for her original Los Angeles owners. Potato Nose, or legally (but not so accurately), Richard Ripardo (Deede, to intimates) had bought the vessel for his construction company that past year. Captain Doug was part of the deal. He said he had signed a one-year contract and the pay was good, but working for Mr. Ripardo...

Doug laughed when Mac asked him how Pumpkin Head fit in. "What a perfect name," he said. "That's top secret – but you'll find out eventually, so I might as well tell you now. His name is George Schwandel, U.S. senator from New Jersey."

Mac asked what brought those two characters together in such a remote spot, but that was information that Doug either did not know or was not willing to share. He did allow us that Ripardo was angling to get a huge freeway contract and that Schwandel must be involved, for as far as the rest of the world was concerned, the good senator was still in Washington.

In less than an hour we were off Isla Partida, the lovely connected island that extends north from Espiritu Santo. The three white beaches of Eclipse Bay sparkled invitingly in the morning sun – a beautiful sight that went totally unnoticed by Potato Nose and Pumpkin Head, even though they had moved their Blood Mary's outside to the cockpit table. They were immersed in their other pastime: gin rummy.

The run from Partida to San Francisco was uneventful and swifter than planned due to a placidly flat sea. Mac suggested a spot to anchor just inside the south arm of San Francisco's main cove. Captain Doug swung the Sea Smasher around and dropped the anchor automatically from the helm.

"If you fellows don't mind, I'll help you inflate the dinghy, but the diving show is yours. Our backup generator needs some attention, and besides, snorkeling and spear-fishing is not my line," said Doug.

It occurred to me that ole Captain Doug was playing it safe, choosing to hide in the bowels of the ship rather than witness the fiasco that would inevitably take place. He quickly stretched out a six-man Avon and started to pump it up, while Mac and I sorted through a deck-box full of masks, snorkels and flippers. We had our own gear, but we thought we might find suitable stuff for the boys.

The plan was for me to swim along the inside of the reef with the men while Mac followed in the dinghy. Potato Nose and Pumpkin Head could get the hang of snorkeling in shallow water and still be able to see a variety of colorful fish.

Seeing Potato and Pumpkin in snorkeling gear was the laugh riot of the year; they were as far out of their tree as the string could stretch. The Three Stooges, Laurel and Hardy, and the Marx Brothers together could not have equaled the comedy of Potato and Pumpkin standing on the swim platform of the Sea Smasher, urging each other to take the plunge. But the absolute show-stopper was Potato's nose, looking more pitted than ever, it completely filled his mask – like an octopus crammed into a very small canning jar.

Mac's lecture on how to breathe and other basics of snorkeling only added pathos to a scene that cost me a bitten tongue for fear of laughing out loud. While our fat friends bobbed on the surface and spit into their masks, we launched the dinghy and, armed with a Hawaiian sling for probing, I led the procession along the rocky point to the harbor entrance. As we pooped along in about six feet of water, the two boys snorted and spewed over the small angelfish that swam right up to their masks. Mac lazily rowed the Avon near enough to our two walruses to give them a sense of security and to offer bits of made-up information about the reef fish.

As we rounded the point, the water dropped off quickly to a rocky bottom. This was the home of many fine fish, including groupers of all sizes. The colder, deeper water had no appeal to Deede, so he asked Mac for a hand to board the dinghy. A derrick would have been more appropriate; hauling a two-hundred-and-fifty-pound jellyfish out of the water is no easy, one-man job.

Unfortunately, Senator Pumpkin was still enchanted and got even more into it when I surfaced from my first dive to report the sighting of a nice grouper in a hole directly below us. Mac handed me a three-banded spear gun. I placed the butt of the gun on my stomach and stretched each band back to its notch at the end of the spear. Mac told the senator to keep his mask in the water and breathe through his snorkel; the water was clear enough that he could float on the surface and watch me go after the fish. I took a deep breath and dove down toward the backside of the sea bass's rock home. With my spear gun aimed straight down, I kicked my flippers twice and glided over the top of the rock. The grouper's head was sticking out of his hole, and before he could sense danger from behind, I fired my spear gun straight down. The spear pierced the fish's head just behind his eyes and, with two or three convulsive tail thrusts, he died.

There was enough line from the gun to the spear so I could surface for a breath by holding the gun with my feet and then dive back to the spear to pull a grouper as long as my leg out of its hole. As I resurfaced, I handed the gun to Mac and he hauled the fish aboard the dinghy before it could attract sharks.

Pumpkin, between blurbs and gasps, relayed the episode back to Potato Nose.

"We got 'im, we got 'im, Deede! Big as a whale! Just look at 'im."

Suddenly, the senator's voice went shrill, "My God, help! I'm surrounded by giant fish!"

He was only twenty yards from the dinghy, and

I don't know if there is a swimming record for the twenty-yard dash, but if there is, Pumpkin Head broke it.

"It's just a school of yellowtail," explained Mac.

"Yellowtail... you mean the same fish we've been catching?"

"Sure," said Mac. "Just stay still and they might swim back underneath you. Makes an easy shot."

"Give me that spear gun," said the senator.

"It's kind of dangerous, and besides, you're turning a little blue," said Mac, wishing he had kept his damn mouth shut.

"Gimme the spear," snorted the senator again. "I didn't come this far to miss shootin' my own fish."

"Oh to hell with it, George – we got enough fish here to feed an army. The damn thing is practically sinking the dinghy," said Potato Nose, sensing the potential for disaster.

But Senator Pumpkin Head was determined, so Mac handed him a loaded spear gun, explained the safety rules, and told him to stay at least thirty feet from the raft.

With murder in his eyes, the senator assumed his battle station. In no time, a school of curious yellowtail passed under me and went to give Pumpkin the once over. With the fish in view, Pumpkin exhaled through the snorkel and then flailed his arms and legs like a wounded hippopotamus as he struggled to line up a shot. I felt the underwater vibration of a spear gun firing. Relieved that nothing had impaled me, I dove in the vicinity of where the senator had fired. Spinning to the bottom was a yellowtail; it was speared in the body, just behind its dorsal fin. Behind the fish trailed the spear gun, tied to the line that ran to the spear. I surfaced, sucked in a lung-full of air and dove again for the fish, hoping to recover the gun. But the yellowtail saw me coming, and though badly wounded, he scurried along the bottom to the deep water beyond.

'That goddamn Pumpkin prick,' I thought as I kicked hard for the surface to refresh my aching lungs – that was my favorite spear gun.

Something weird was going on. Mac was in the water towing the senator back to the Avon while Potato Nose was throwing a screaming fit.

"What happened," I shouted. I could not believe that such a wild scene had developed during a less-than-one-minute dive.

"I thought he'd speared himself," yelled Mac. "It's something worse. Get the hell back in the dinghy!"

Mac climbed aboard on the other side, and together, we pulled the unconscious senator on board. Potato's fit had escalated, so Mac ordered him to lie down by the dead fish and shut up.

The senator looked dead. Blood ran from his nose and mouth, but there was no evidence of a wound. Mac wiped the blood from the senator's mouth with his tee shirt and tried mouth-to-mouth resuscitation. After a few breaths, Pumpkin started bleeding again – even from his ears. Mac finally stopped. Thank God, for the sight was about to make me puke.

I started rowing, but I couldn't look at ole Pumpkin and his fleshy body, clumps of black and gray hair, and rolled-back eyes. It was the second dead body that I had ever seen. Fortunately, I didn't have to tango with this one.

The First Life of Andy McCurdy

I just rowed hard for the Sea Smasher. Potato Nose sat obediently, shaking and occasionally farting by the dead grouper.

I asked Mac again what had happened.

"I'm not sure," he answered. "He fired the spear gun and then he sank. When he resurfaced, he never exhaled. Swimming towards him I saw blood oozing from the tip of his snorkel. I thought maybe he'd speared himself."

Mac paused and then he said, "Something big must have burst. Maybe his whole heart exploded. All that gin and then struggling to shoot the fish was just too much."

"He hit a yellowtail," I said. "Got it in the tail and then he dropped the gun. I tried to dive for it, but the fish towed it into deep water."

As we neared the stern of the Sea Smasher, I thought of Captain Doug and how his quiet solitude in the engine room would soon end.

After boarding, Potato's composure returned a bit. "Is that asshole really dead?" were Potato's first remarks concerning the condition of his dear, old, top-secret drinking pal.

"Where's Blackburn? We got big problems," shouted Potato. "You bastards have just killed the likely next vice president of the United States."

The grotesque humor of poor, dead Pumpkin as a candidate for the vice presidency did not dampen the instant offense Mac took to Potato Head's remark. Mac pulled him backwards over the cocktail table by his hair, and bent his neck over the side so hard that I thought we might have another corpse on our hands.

"I'm sorry, I'm sorry. For Christ's sake, don't get so tough about it," gurgled Potato as Mac turned his head loose. "You don't understand. Schwandel is not here, I mean, he's not supposed to be here. He's in Washington and, dead or alive, we got to get him back there."

"You probably have a better chance getting him there dead," said Mac, cynically. "But our first chore is to get him out of the dinghy. Got any ideas, Captain?"

"Well, if he were a big fish, like a marlin, we could gaff him and use the electric hoist to lift him aboard, but that might rip his body up a bit. Perhaps the best plan is to use the stern davits and hoist the entire dinghy onto the aft deck," thought Blackburn out loud.

Mac agreed, and ten minutes later, the dinghy carrying Senator Pumpkin was aboard. Then the real chore began. Pumpkin's body was big and mushy, and lifting him required each of us to grab a limb. I was assigned a leg. I knew that touching him would make me puke; not enough time had gone by since my last encounter with a pulpy body. This one was not dancing with me, nor did it have a chance to bite me, but it still made me puke. That was enough to trigger the same reaction from Potato Nose, so the hauling stopped while Blackburn got a bucket of water and a mop. After the cleanup, we more or less dragged the corpse below-deck to a full-sized bathtub.

As the captain counted cadence, "One, two, three – lift," we let the senator slip, like a giant balloon full of jelly, into the bathtub.

Back on deck, after attending to some personal hygiene, Mac resumed the conversation, "Getting a body out of Mexico is no small problem. You may think you know all about red tape, but you haven't seen anything yet."

"There's going to be no red tape, no Mexican officials, no nothing. Schwandel is going back to D.C. where he can die in his own bathtub. Any other way and we got an international problem of the first magnitude," barked Potato.

The First Life of Andy McCurdy

"What do you mean, 'we got problems'," snapped Mac. "I'd say you got problems, and we wish you the best of luck. Let's get this barge headed back to La Paz, Doug. We've had enough of Mr. Ripardo's bullshit."

"Wait, wait," pleaded Deede. "I'll level with you guys. This problem goes all the way to the top, I mean to the White House. Campaign financing and freeway contracts, Senator Schwandel was the conduit. If he's found dead here with me, the balloon blows up. The shit hits the fan."

"Sounds like that's about what should happen to those crooked bastards in Washington," said Mac, revealing both his lack of sympathy and his political leaning.

"Look," said Deede in a more controlled tone, "this isn't about one political party, it's about our country, and right now, it would be bad for America to have a stinking scandal. Just trust me. Help me get the senator back to San Diego and you guys will never be a part of this problem again."

"How and why would we possibly help?" asked Mac, skeptically.

"We need crew to get my boat back to San Diego. That's the how. And the why is that I'll give you one hundred grand for your troubles. Like it or not, you're already involved in the death of a U.S. senator. Your credentials for guiding novices on diving expeditions might become an issue, and who knows what else."

"Sounds like you're bribing me, Ripardo," said Mac, looking like he might bend Potato's neck over the table again.

"All I'm saying is that I will provide you with a written guarantee that you are absolved of any part of what happened today – regardless of what happens after San Diego. It will come from the top of our government. Plus, your hundred grand will be delivered tax-free in any form you like."

"You're thinking pretty fast and talking mighty big for a guy who was babbling like the village idiot just a few minutes ago," said Mac.

"How long to get us to San Diego?" said Potato Nose to Captain Blackburn, ignoring Mac's last remark.

Looking rather ashen, Doug said, "With reasonable weather and no refueling, maybe fifty hours from the cape."

"OK. Let's haul for La Paz, top off the fuel tanks, get a dinghy full of ice, and head for Cabo," said Potato.

"What's all the ice for?" I asked without thinking.

"We got a dead senator stashed in a bathtub – we need a lot of ice to keep him fresh," answered Ripardo.

Mac and I putted our dinghy back to the Sumac without exchanging a word. I knew Mac was conjuring up an explanation for Mom. I wasn't sure what he would say, but I knew it had to be damn good.

Mac told the story straight as Mom listened without much change in expression – except for the mouth-to-mouth part.

When Mac was through, there seemed to be a long silence. Finally, Mom said rather quietly, "Do you remember the last words I said to you before you left this morning, 'Please try to stay out of trouble?'

"Now, less than eight hours later, you boys return from what should have been an uneventful diving trip, and what do you report? Stories about catching a big fish or stories about the funny characters you spent the day with? Oh, no! You guys slink back here and tell me about your involvement

The First Life of Andy McCurdy

in the death of a U.S. senator, and that, for your next adventure, you plan to haul a corpse illegally out of Mexico. And what are your pals doing now? Oh, nothing much, just out buying a ton of crushed ice to keep the dead senator from rotting!

"Now, is there anything else that either one of you would like to add, or does that pretty well sum it up?"

"Well, I didn't say we would do it, but I did think it would be a way of picking up a new propeller and enough money to pay for a college education," Mac added in a tone that lacked the smallest drop of conviction.

Another long pause was broken by Mom asking, "Think it's worth it, Mac? What are you going to do? You'll never be able to criticize Nixon again. Doc's going to laugh you under the table."

After an even longer silence, Mom continued, "Well, I'll tell you what, if you are going to do it, I'm going, too. I didn't want to tell you, but I think I've got my bladder infection back. I need a check-up and some antibiotics. Doc and Lizzie got back in port today, and they invited Joey and Annie to go specimen collecting with them tomorrow. Andy, you can go, too, or you can stay here and guard the boat. We'll fly back in three days, one hundred thousand dollars richer, but morally bankrupt."

"Holy cats, Mom. You think as fast as Potato Head," I said, but regretted it immediately.

Chapter Fifteen

Two hours later, Mom and Mac roared out of La Paz Harbor on the Sea Smasher while I heated up some pasta with pesto for dinner. That night, Joey and Annie wanted to hear the graphic details of Pumpkin Head's last dive. Telling them probably wasn't a good idea. It was a dark night and Mom and Mac were gone; not the right time for a scary story. No one slept in the open cockpit that night. We locked all the hatches and bunched together on the v-births in the forepeak cabin.

The next morning Joey and Annie engrossed themselves in backgammon, a game that every member of our family excelled in – except me. Doc and Lizzie were to pick the kids up for a day's outing to Espiritu Santo, so I decided to head for the local supermarket.

As soon as I jumped into the dinghy, Ole Yellow started running down the dock to greet me. I had never had a dog of my own and I didn't start this friendship, but for some reason he just took to me. Before I knew it, I had a pal. There must have been fifty thousand street dogs in La Paz, and all of them looked pretty much the same, but Yellow wasn't quite as scrawny as the rest and he was, well, yellow.

We took off walking together along the main street that ran parallel to the harbor. As we passed the veranda outside the Los Arcos Hotel, I glanced up at two people sitting at a table right off the street.

My heart jumped out of my chest! Sitting there plain as day were the weird couple that I had seen on the yacht club dock the night before we left. That close up in the light of day, there was no question about it. I tried to act nonchalant: pulling on the stick in Yellow's mouth and pretending I didn't see them. Praying they didn't recognize me, I hurried around the corner.

When we got to the *tienda* my knees were still knocking and all kinds of thoughts were racing through my mind. Maybe I should go to the police and tell them the whole story? Maybe they would make an arrest. But an arrest for what? Being on a San Diego dock two months ago? No way. Besides my Spanish stunk; they'd only laugh at me. Maybe I should go back to the Los Arcos and take another look. No, that was them. There was no question about it.

I could find a gun, but where? This was Mexico – foreigners aren't allowed to have guns. If they get caught with one, it's a sure trip to the slammer. On second thought, maybe I should do something that put me in jail. I'd be safe there. No, that's not true. No kid my age is safe in a Mexican prison. I'd read enough about that to curl your hair...

After buying the provisions from the supermarket, I walked a different route back to the dock. I could see Ole Yellow standing guard on the shore as I rowed the dinghy back to the Sumac. My mind was still racing. I had no doubt that I had just seen the couple from the yacht club. There was no mistaking his busted face and her squatty frame and red hair. 'What great timing,' I thought: 'Mac and Mom were a million miles away and Doc and Lizzie probably wouldn't come back until after dark.'

"Of course I see the kid. So what," said Bruno.

"You don't get it, do you, lame brain? That's the kid that spoke to us when we were pulling the dinghy onto the dock in San Diego. He's the only living soul that saw us that night," said Angel.

"So weeks later a kid walks in front of us and you know for sure that he's the same brat. Even if he was –"

"Shut up," interrupted Angel. "It's the same boy, and he recognized us. Get off your ass and follow him. Don't lose him and don't let him see you," she ordered.

Bruno slinked away on the trail that eventually led him to Sawyer's dock. His dim brain registered when he watched Andy paddle back to a K-50.

"Maybe Angel had it straight. That kid in San Diego was on the same kind of sailboat. I better go back and give her a report," he muttered to himself.

"What in hell are you doing back here? I told you to watch that kid," barked Angel when Bruno entered her hotel room.

"He got on a K-50 anchored off Sawyer's. She's flying a San Diego Yacht Club burgee," he reported.

Angel grabbed her briefcase off the bed and pulled out a SDYC directory. She always carried numerous West Coast yacht club directories to aid her in her nasty business. In minutes, she had identified three K-50s.

"What's the name of the boat the kid got on?" she asked.

"I didn't notice," said Bruno, sheepishly.

"You dumb shit! Go the hell back and find out!" shouted Angel.

Twenty minutes later, Bruno returned with the news that the K-50 was named the Sumac, and that, except for a yellow dog on the dock, the kid was onboard alone.

Angel busied herself with the directory again, then read aloud, "'Sumac, owned by Elliot and Susan McCurdy.'

"So where are the parents? Go rustle up Woogie and have him get the dope on what's going on with the Sumac," commanded Angel.

Besides being an odd jobs guy, Woogie specialized in knowing all the anchorage scuttlebutt. He had been on Angel's payroll since she first started her dirty work in La Paz.

Chapter Sixteen

I popped in a tape of Bobby Darin's "Beyond the Sea" – one of Mom's favorites. I thought it might settle my nerves a little, but it only made me feel worse. When I had woken up that morning, I had been looking forward to a day of solitude, but after seeing that couple, solitude was the last thing I wanted. I thought about getting on the radio telephone, but the whole world could listen in, including the bad guys. Besides, Doc wouldn't be listening to his radio. Then I remembered the danger signal that Doc had invented, so I hoisted the club burgee upside-down on the port yardarm halyard.

Afterwards, I stretched out on the cockpit bench and listened to a Peter, Paul and Mary tape. I scanned the sky, but it was still too light to find Arcturus. Besides, clouds were moving in, and it would be overcast by evening. There wouldn't be any stars – a dark, dark night was coming on. I could barely see Ole Yellow on the shore. Like a sentinel, he always seemed to be on watch for me. I wished that I had brought him back on board; at least then I would have had some company. My parents were a thousand miles away. Doc and Lizzie were gone for the day and maybe the night. Even the kids would have been welcome companionship. It was only six o'clock, but it was getting dark fast. The air was chilly, so I pulled a blanket over myself, but I couldn't stop shaking. I didn't like being alone; I was scared. I thought that in a little while I'd get up and row to shore. Maybe I'd walk around where there were lots of people for a while, and I'd bring Ole Yellow back with me for sure.

"Now try to get it straight, Lame Brain. We're going to pull off one more caper and then that's it. In the next few days we'll spot an easy mark, trail them to Cabo and make our move. We've been lucky so far. Our trail is pretty clean, but there are two people who could hurt us: this kid on the K-50 and Woogie. They gotta go. Soon as that's over, we concentrate on our next pigeons. After that, we're rich," said Angel.

"Getting rid of Woogie's no problem, but doin' a kid... I don't know about that," said Bruno.

"Look, that kid is the one that could really finger us. He saw us. He saw our dinghy and the timing fits with the hit. He knows that we are here in La Paz, and he'll be blowing the whistle soon. One less kid isn't going to make this world any different, so don't go soft on me now," growled Angel.

"What's your plan," sniffled Bruno.

"The kid is alone now, so we take him tonight. Woogie drops us off on the K-50 and rows back to shore. We jump the kid and set up a butane leak. Standard procedure, we've got the maneuver down cold," said Angel.

"But what if the kid sees us coming. He'll sound an alarm and the whole harbor will fall on our ass," cried Bruno.

"It'll be dark by six o'clock. We know how to sneak onto a boat. He won't hear or see a thing until it's too late."

"But blowing up another boat – that trick is gettin' old," whimpered Bruno.

"People just get careless with their butane, it happens all the time. Kids are worse than grown-ups. They never think about safety. No, this is a natural. When it's all over, bingo! One less sailboat and one less kid. We hunker down for a few days and then we're back to work," said Angel.

As Angel had instructed, Bruno and Woogie found some old rubber fenders in a scrap pile in Sawyer's yard. The fenders would be hung along the side of Woogie's rowboat so that it could silently touch the Sumac's hull.

Just after dark, Woogie rowed Bruno and Angel to the bow of the sailboat. They slipped aboard and Woogie returned to shore to wait for a signal. On seeing no sign of Andy, Angel and Bruno figured he was in the main cabin.

Even though Angel looked squat and awkward, she could move as nimbly as a cat. She crept down one side of the Sumac as Bruno went down the other, slowly working their way to the stern cockpit.

Bruno had his knife ready. He wasn't good at much, but he could throw a knife with deadly accuracy. He could also use it to kill quickly at close range.

The plan was for Angel to enter the cabin first, jump Andy and take him down before he could move. Bruno would be right behind her with his knife, ready to back her up if needed.

It's hard to believe, but while listening to that tape I fell asleep. That was a stupid mistake, and I awoke to the horror of my life. Worse than being

The First Life of Andy McCurdy

entangled with the decaying Mexican fisherman; worse than dead Pumpkin Head; I looked up to see Shovel Face. It was too late to struggle; he had covered my mouth with duct tape and I was yanked down below.

His girlfriend prodded me in the ribs with her pistol and said, "Thanks, kid. Sneaking onto boats is our profession, but you really made it easy for us."

When they pushed me down on the starboard bunk and pulled off the duct tape, I was sure my life was about to end. They weren't arguing about if they would kill me – they were squabbling about how and when.

I offered up some of my own ideas, like how killing me would prove nothing, but they weren't listening. They just snarled at me like two wolves ready to rip apart a fresh kill.

The woman, apparently named Angel, asked me what I was doing on the dock in San Diego that night.

I stupidly answered, "Getting the boat ready for departure."

"Thanks for the confirmation, kid. We wouldn't want to waste our time knocking off the wrong boy. You just signed your own death warrant," said Angel with a smirk.

"Wait, I know where there's a buried treasure. It's probably worth millions. My parents and I – we found it a few days ago. That's where we banged up our propeller."

"Shut up, kid," said Angel as she smacked my head with her pistol barrel.

She ordered her partner, Bruno, to take our dinghy ashore and take care of Woogie and Ole Yellow.

"When you get back, it'll be late enough to do our job here," she said.

After Bruno left I could almost feel the atmosphere change.

"I've always liked young boys – maybe we should kill Bruno, then you and I can take up together," she said with a shit-eating smile that flaunted her crooked yellow teeth.

"That's a great idea!" I said, sensing a slight reprieve from my death sentence.

But then she said, "Take off your clothes, kid."

"No, no... Please don't do this," I pleaded.

"Shut up, kid – you want to die now?"

As I took off my shirt, she said, "Take your shorts off."

I thought about lunging for her pistol, but she never got careless with it. Before I could blink my eyes, she was stark naked. Now I'm no connoisseur of the female body, but this was no Venus, not even a Mrs. Robinson. She was squatty and rather muscular and had sagging breasts. In a nutshell, she looked better with her clothes on.

She wasted no time doing things to me that had never been done before.

"Please, lady," I shouted, "just shoot me. Do it now."

I really wasn't up for that either, but damn, I hated myself. It was disgusting; that bitch had made me hard. She pushed me back on the bunk and jumped on top of me, keeping the pistol aimed straight at my temple. She started humping me like a wild animal. As she moaned and groaned I was sure she'd pull the trigger and blow my head off. But at the end, she just lay on top of me, sweating like the pig she was.

So this would be my first (and last), I thought to myself. Not exactly what I had dreamed. So when did you first do it with a woman? Well, I was almost

The First Life of Andy McCurdy

seventeen, when this ugly, middle-aged woman raped me just before she shot me dead.

It got to be later, and for some reason, I was still alive. I felt a dinghy bump against the hull of the Sumac. It was Bruno.

"What did you do with Woogie?" asked Angel.

"We took a trip toward the airport on his old Vespa. Told him we needed a couple Aeronaves tickets to Mazatlan. Woogie had an unfortunate accident on the way. We stopped for a leak at the edge of town. I was going to stick him in the back, but I just waited for him to finish and when he turned around I slit his throat from ear to ear. Guess I really caught him by surprise," said Bruno

"Oh, I'm sure you did – you're getting real good at that. What did you do with his body?" questioned Angel.

"No problem, just tossed him into a real deep ditch off the dirt road. Even covered him up with weeds," answered Bruno proudly.

"And the dog?" asked Angel.

"Ate a bad wiener and crawled under the old boat storage shed in back of Sawyer's. He won't be coming out."

"Well, what do you know. We're down to one last witness and he's sittin' here, right in front of us, looking like his eyeballs are about to pop out of his head," said Angel.

That was true. I was scared shitless, but I was also mad as hell. Mad at myself for not making a move when there was only one of them and one gun aimed at me. Mad at them for killing my buddy, Ole Yellow. Mad enough to overcome my fear!

I guessed their plan was to blow me and the Sumac up in smoke the same way as they did with Tom and Rosa Bryce on the Wind Song. My time was up, and I knew it.

Bruno was sitting on the bunk across from me. He pulled his knife out of the leather sheath that he wore on his belt. He put it on the table, in plain sight, like he wanted me to see it – daring me to make a grab for it. I knew nothing about knives, but this one looked like a dagger or maybe a stiletto. One thing for sure was that it was wicked looking. Bruno kept spinning it with his finger. Every time it stopped the pointed blade was aimed directly at me. This little game seemed to amuse Bruno; each time his whirling knife came to a stop, he chortled a little. Perhaps he was practicing a ritual that lifted him into a psychopathic frenzy that climaxed with the act of killing at close range.

He just stared at me through his watery eyes. His kinky yellow hair hung over his distorted face, and his sordid grin displayed his scraggy teeth. The horror of seeing Bruno up close would normally have been enough to make me completely lose it, bowels and bladder included. But fear no longer controlled me. Instead I focused both physically and mentally for the attack.

'How strange,' I thought, 'in all my life I had never been in a fight, and now the first one would be for my life. A maniac with a long knife was preparing to decapitate me! God be with me and give me the courage and the strength to prevail,' I prayed.

I would go for the arm that held the knife. I would gouge his eyes, kick his groin, do whatever I could to hurt him. I knew it would not be enough; lurking behind him would be the red-headed bitch, ready to end the fight with her pistol.

Time was running out but, weirdly, time stood still. Angel had her gun and Bruno had his dagger, but no one seemed to move.

It flashed through my mind that I had seen my last glorious sunset, seen my last look at Arcturus and my last dream about Maggie. I was facing death, but I wasn't frightened anymore. That bastard had killed my pal, Ole Yellow, and the disgusting bitch had forced her repulsive self on my body. I hated them both and I wanted to kill them, but I had to make the first move, and I had to make it fast or I'd be history.

Under the bunk I was lying on was a three-banded spear gun. I could reach it with my right hand, but by the time I could pull it out and cock the rubber bands, I'd be full of bullet holes.

Ever since Angel had forced me onto the bunk, I'd been practicing in my mind what to do. I would grab the spear gun with my right hand, hold the pistol butt to my stomach, and then grab all three bands and pull them back to the locking notches on the spear. I'd practiced that maneuver in the water when I needed to get a quick shot off at a fish, so I knew how to do it, but I would still need a little luck to hit all three notches simultaneously.

I'd go for the bitch with my spear gun first because she had the pistol; then I'd fight off Bruno any way I could. It was not a good plan and the odds were not in my favor, but anything was better than just waiting for Bruno to slit my throat. Something had to distract them just for a second or two so I would have a chance to make a move.

I had no idea that the Sirius had just returned and was at anchor only a few hundred yards away. Doc had tried to reach me by radio, but it wasn't on, so Joey had asked if he could take Doc's dinghy over to see what I was doing. When he got within range, Joey noticed something strange: the yacht club burgee was hanging upside-down from the port yardarm.

Remember that I had always said that Joey was

a smart little guy? Well, he proved it again. He instantly knew that there was big trouble aboard the Sumac. He thought about heading back to get Doc, but somehow he sensed that his big brother needed help right away.

"Hey, Andy, we're back. You ready for a late supper?" hailed Joey.

"Who the hell is that," said Bruno as Angel looked through the port cabin window and saw Joey not one hundred feet away.

"Go up and give that kid a friendly greeting. Tell him Andy's hurt himself and you are looking after him. Invite him aboard. Then grab the little bastard when he gets alongside and break his neck," ordered Angel.

Obediently, Bruno grabbed his knife and went up onto the cockpit.

Trying to sound friendly, he said, "Hi, kid. I need your help. Come on aboard."

Joey moved to the bow of the dinghy to hand Bruno a line as Angel took a step up the companionway to the cockpit to be sure Bruno did his job.

'It's now or never,' I thought.

"Go Joey, go! Get out of here!" I screamed as I made my move for the spear gun.

Angel whirled back at me with pistol in hand. It had been the first time that she had let me out of her sight.

All the spear gun's bands snapped cleanly into their notches, and I fired the spear directly at her gut. It was a clean hit. The spear impaled her just below her rib cage and embedded itself in the bulkhead directly behind her. Blood spurted from her belly like a fountain.

For a second, Angel gazed at me in disbelief.

She tried to raise her pistol, but her body slumped over sideways as if she was doing a cartwheel with the spear holding her up at the midsection. She dangled on the bulkhead, bleeding to death.

I grabbed Angel's pistol and rushed to help Joey. I heard a smacking sound like a bat hitting a softball. The image of Bruno hurling his knife at Joey pierced my mind as I raced up the companionway. I knew that murdering bastard had hurt my brother and I was in a blind rage to retaliate. A split second later I saw the damnedest sight of my life. Hanging over the cockpit lifeline like a sack of oats was Shovel Face.

Wise little Joey. When he had spotted the upside-down burgee, he knew that there was trouble and he had quickly made a plan of his own. When Bruno asked him to hand up the line, Joey pretended to cooperate, but in his other hand he held Doc's fish bat – a weapon similar to ours, but heavier and with a longer steel spike at its end.

When Bruno leaned over to grab the line, Joey swung the bat in a roundhouse motion and impaled the eight inch steel spike into Bruno's skull. Bruno didn't make a sound; he just hung there looking as if he had grown an elephant trunk.

I jumped into the dinghy to comfort Joey.

He kept saying, "I only meant to knock him out! I forgot about the spike!"

I held Joey in my arms and let him sob.

"You did the right thing, bro. You saved my life. You saved your own life. You saved our boat. You're a hero."

"Did I kill him, Andy?" he cried.

"Probably," I answered, "but just in time. In a few seconds it would have been us lying on the floor, instead of those murdering rats."

Doc knew something was wrong. Not having a second dinghy, he pulled anchor, powered the Sirius over, and, with bumpers in place, he docked side-by-side with the Sumac. Lizzie and Annie secured the lines as Doc leaped from his boat. He was with us in the dinghy in an instant. After seeing that we were unhurt, he climbed aboard the Sumac to assess the battle damage.

Reappearing from the galley, breathing hard but trying to appear cool, Doc said, "Looks like a decisive victory for our side. You boys don't fool around. The lady below deck appears to have had some major stomach problems. A spear through the aorta was just too much for her to digest. As for this ugly chap, it took a mighty good shot to find his little, pea-sized brain with the gaff. Congratulations to both of you. You've saved yourselves and rid the world of two despicable killers."

"They've done more killing, Doc," I said. "I heard the man called Bruno say that he killed Woogie – slit his throat from ear to ear, and then he stuffed the body in a ditch off a side road near the airport. Worse than that, he said he poisoned my pal, Ole Yellow."

Chapter Seventeen

La Paz Harbor was lit up like a Christmas tree. Searchlights, sirens, police and spectators were all converging on the Sumac. Doc had radioed a distress call on his portable VHF radio just before he had boarded the Sumac. The whole world had heard his broadcast.

I must have been in shock because I remember only a few things vividly – the rest blurred into one major nightmare. I remembered firing the spear at Angel and watching her swing her pistol right at me. I knew I had hit her, but I thought I was just a second too late. I remembered her lips curled into a nasty sneer as she sighted her pistol at my chest. I remembered blood drooling out of the corners of her mouth as her upper body slumped over, but the spear kept her pinned to the wall like a mounted trophy.

Then I remembered sitting next to Joey in the dinghy. I had imagined the worst but I saw Bruno draped over the stern lifeline with the fish bat stuck in his head instead.

Finally, I remembered Doc rushing Joey and me aboard the Sirius as a patrol boat arrived with two Spanish-looking but English-speaking men. They identified themselves as U.S. federal agents working undercover in conjunction with the Mexican government.

Doc invited them to step aboard. Paul, the agent in charge, began, "We knew these guys were smuggling cocaine and we were almost certain that they had killed the Bryces."

"If you knew all that, why didn't you nab them before they killed again?" asked Doc.

"Frankly, we were using them to lead us to bigger fish. A few days ago they took possession of a new rubber dinghy; probably stashed with cocaine. We tracked the guy who delivered it back to Mexico City, and a bust was made there yesterday," said Paul.

"So you risked the lives of these boys by letting killers roam around loose," barked Doc.

"Not really, at least not on purpose. We made a mistake. We expected that they would target another boat departing for the U.S. Their involvement with you guys came up out of the blue. It's just not consistent with their previous activity and we were caught off guard," replied the agent.

"I can tell you how it's consistent! They wanted to get rid of me because I was the only person who saw them the night the Bryces were murdered," I blubbered.

I filled the agent in with all the details of the night on the San Diego Yacht Club dock and being spotted by Angel and Bruno that morning in front of the Los Arcos.

"That's an incredible coincidence. You've been living with an awful nightmare. But I'll tell you what, your testimony is sure going to make closing this case easy work," said Agent Paul.

"What's that going to entail?" piped in Doc.

"Tell you later. You boys pull away and take up anchor nearby. The Sumac is off-limits until noon tomorrow. We'll do an inspection with the Mexican police. After that, we'll do a complete cleanup job. We'll also need to conduct a more formal interview with the boys tomorrow. The Mexican police will want to be involved. No big deal, maybe we can do it right here. Then there will be the press; they have wind of a big story already, but for security reasons, we're holding them off until tomorrow," answered Agent Paul.

After the agents departed, I remember feeling dazed, but not remorseful. I needed no consoling for what I had done. I figured that I had rid the world of a nasty psychopathic killer and I wouldn't hesitate to do it again.

Joey didn't need much consolation, either. I don't know if it had all sunk in yet, but he responded well to the praise Doc and Lizzie gave him. After a little supper, Doc gave us some sort of "relaxing" pill. The only recollection I have after that was of hearing a tape of "Raindrops Keep Falling on My Head" – Annie's favorite song. She had stayed in the background through the ordeal, but still tried every way she could to give comfort to Joey and me.

It seemed like no time at all before my lights went out. Doc's pill had scored a knockout.

Chapter Eighteen

The next morning in Los Angeles, Leonard Peters was going through his morning ritual. Dressing immaculately was a compulsion, and the process was taking longer than usual when the entrance buzzer of his apartment house sounded.

"Who is it," demanded Peters.

"Special Agents Kelly and Navone, F.B.I. We'd like a word with you."

"Sorry, I'm unavailable. Try my office this afternoon," answered Peters.

"Listen, Peters. Your friends, Angel and Bruno, had some bad luck last night. You'll want to know the details, so just buzz open this door or we'll bust our way in and have your fat ass on the floor in about ten seconds."

Peters didn't answer, but the door lock clicked open and in seconds the agents were rapping on his apartment door.

Kelly and Navone moved through the apartment like two hunters, while Peters stood barefoot in the center of his living room in candy-striped boxers and a powder-blue silk shirt. Then Kelly began the interrogation as Navone continued a detailed inspection of the apartment.

"Yep, your old friends, Angel and Bruno, had a really bad night," started Kelly, as he pushed his face up close to Peters'.

The First Life of Andy McCurdy

"Damned if they didn't get themselves killed. Made the mistake of irritating a couple of young boys who blew 'em away with a spear gun and a fish bat."

"So what's that got to do with me," demanded Peters.

"A whole bunch," said Kelly, grabbing Peters by his necktie and yanking it tight enough to choke him.

"Your ass is grass, man. Last night in La Paz, shortly after Angel's unsuccessful attempt to digest a fishspear, our people found a notebook in her hotel room. That notebook has enough information to hang you by the balls, but the frosting on the cake is a tape of your last meeting with her. You know – the one where you reviewed how the Bryces were abducted and murdered, and then planned another Baja drug job – you even ordered a contract on Bruno and Woogie.

"Yep, you're a real bastard, Peters. Even Angel hated your guts. Chances are that, had she not got her tummy stuck on the sharp end of a fishspear, she would have put you down for good. Too bad she didn't get the chance, but that would have cheated us of this pleasure."

Tugging Peters' tie even tighter, Kelly continued, "You see, Agent Navone and me, we see a lot of messed-up people, especially kids. Then we see you living high on the hog in this swanky apartment, with enough blue suits to fill a men's store and drivin' around in a big Mercedes. Well, it just don't sit right with us. The system just moves too slow. It lets rats like you sit on death row for fifteen years, eatin' good food, writin' a book, and pretty soon enough time goes by that people forget what a worthless piece of slime you really are."

Peters tried to talk, but Kelly pulled his tie so tight that all he could do was gurgle.

"No, we don't want to hear any bullshit from you, Peters. Why don't you make a move and make it easy for us to blow some holes through your nice blue shirt?"

"I got an idea," said Navone. "No sense wasting bullets on this piece of crap. I found a hammer in a kitchen drawer; it's perfect for the old toe-smashing trick."

"Hey, we haven't busted toes for a long time," replied Kelly.

"But, maybe we make a deal. He tells us who he answers to and we let the locals take him in with full protection," suggested Navone. "But, on the other hand, let's bust one of pecker-head's toes as a partial payback for all the people he's hurt."

"Great idea," said Kelly. Then he yanked Peters around by his tie and slammed him down on a straight-backed chair.

Navone locked Peters' arms behind the chair with handcuffs as Kelly strapped his ankles to the chair legs with a couple of beautiful Countess Mara neckties.

"I need a little practice," said Navone. "Toss me a walnut from that dish."

Kelly complied and Navone put the walnut an inch away from Peters' big toe. Then he swung the hammer like a logger splitting wood and the walnut shattered into a million pieces.

"Man, that tile floor will be perfect for making goo out of toes," said Navone as he took aim for one of Peters' little toes.

"No, go for a big toe first, makes a better target – but wait, maybe pecker-head doesn't want his toes turned into ketchup. Maybe he'd like to tell us who the big cheese is," suggested Kelly.

"We don't need to know that right now," pleaded Navone. "We owe it to all the people he's hurt. Let's just bust one toe! Then he'll be answering questions faster than we can ask 'em."

"Well, what do you think Peters? Should I let my partner crunch some toes, or would you rather answer a few questions and be able to walk out of here?"

Sweat was streaming down Peters' face when Navone smashed another walnut to smithereens.

Peters' eyes closed as if he were contemplating what to say. His jaw muscles flexed. Then, in a harsh whisper he said, "Ripardo, Richard Ripardo... I'm not going down alone. That son of a bitch is going with me."

His jaw muscles flexed again and there was a slight crunching sound. Kelly knew instantly what it was. He squeezed Peters' cheeks to open his mouth and he rammed his fingers in, but he was too late. Peters had crushed a small glass vial between his teeth, releasing a deadly poison. His body convulsed once, then stiffened like a ramrod. Before Kelly could pull his fingers from his mouth, Peters slumped forward. His heart had stopped.

"Shit," said Kelly. "He had that damn thing in his mouth the whole time. I should have checked."

"Wouldn't have done any good," said Navone. "Rats like Peters know that they have no place to go. In their dirty business, the middlemen are expendable. If they don't move up the chain, they face the music. All they got left are enemies, and eventually they get hit, either by us or one of their own. The bottom line is that this bastard got off easy."

"Call the meat-wagon and start packing any stuff that might be useful. I'll get the wheels turning on Richard Ripardo," said Kelly. "Maybe we got a shot at a big fish."

On the way out, Navone spotted a framed photograph on Peters' desk. It was a picture of Peters standing on the fantail deck of a luxurious yacht. A well-dressed man was shaking Peters' hand as if he were giving his congratulations. The picture was taken from a dock so it showed the boat's stern, but the boat's name was not quite distinguishable. Navone could just barely make out that there were two words, both starting with "S", and the home port which appeared to be Marina del Rey.

"Looks like Peters traveled with fancy company," said Navone.

"Yeah, stick the photo in your briefcase. We'll get it checked out later," said Kelly.

Chapter Nineteen

Doc's knockout pill was hard to shake off, but after breakfast my head cleared enough so that I could tell Doc the whole story about my encounter with Angel. The retelling of that rabid bitch humping me was enough to make me puke. But Doc said that I had done the right thing. If I had made a move for her gun, I would not have been there to tell the story. In fact, blowing my brains out might have added to her lecherous thrill.

Doc dug into his medical supplies and fished out some pills.

"Take one of these now, just to be safe. It's enough penicillin to kill any bug before it gets started – in the military we called 'em 'no sweat' pills."

As I swallowed Doc's horse pill, I looked through the porthole to see Agent Paul coming alongside. He'd had a successful night. They had found a rubber dinghy rolled-up into a neat package in Angel's hotel room. The inflatable sides contained at least thirty-five kilos of cocaine worth well over a million dollars on the wholesale market. Angel's notebook supplied enough evidence to remove any doubt about Bruno and Angel's involvement in the murders of Tom and Rosa Bryce.

More importantly, Angel had carelessly left contact information for her boss in Los Angeles. As a result, a key bust had been made early that morning.

"Angel must have hated this guy. She had taped their last meeting. The details about murdering the Bryces and plans for the next cocaine smuggle were there – clear evidence for a real hanging.

"Best of all, her boss got caught with his pants down and no time to hide anything. He croaked during the arrest, but not before blabbing some clues that could lead to the guy at the very top. He's probably head of a major bank or president of his country club. Whoever he is, he'll be clean as a whistle – a real big shot with more connections in high places than a phone company, and more money than Fort Knox – but he's going down. It may take a giant cannon to do the job but eventually we are going to hang him," stated Agent Paul with total conviction.

Paul also reported that the Mexican police had traced the tracks of a Vespa down a dirt road just off the airport highway. Bruno had done a sloppy job of hiding poor Woogie's body. The fact that Woogie was practically decapitated confirmed the story I had overheard Bruno telling to Angel.

As predicted, the police arrived, and for three hours Joey and I answered questions. The men were polite but thorough, sometimes asking us the same questions different ways. Joey and I had no trouble keeping our stories straight, because it all was the truth. Well, almost. Our answers about Mom and Mac's whereabouts were kind of evasive. We said that Mom was having a medical problem and wanted to see her doctor in San Diego, and the owner of the yacht, the Sea Smasher, had offered her a fast trip home. The Mexican police worked hard for more details, but we offered none. Fortunately, there were no questions about a dead senator.

After the police left, Agent Paul confided that he was fully aware that Senator Schwandel was packed in ice aboard the Sea Smasher and that U.S. agents would be at the customs dock to greet them. There would be no problems. The feds had a plan to discreetly escort Schwandel's body back to Washington, D.C. Those orders had come from the highest authorities.

"Oh, Andy, one thing more. I'd like you to come with me for one final bit of business. Doc's already gone to run an errand on shore, so you can get a ride back with him," said Paul.

We powered to the dock and walked on a back street in the general direction of the Los Arcos. In the middle of the block we turned into an arcade and entered an open door that led to a dank little waiting room that looked like part of a doctor's office with no signs. I sat on a couch with Agent Paul, expecting an explanation, but he offered nothing. Then the backroom door burst open, and my eyes bulged out of my head. Sitting there with Doc, big as life, was Ole Yellow! I ran for him, and we hugged and kissed and slobbered all over each other.

"Easy," said Doc. "He's still a sick dog, but he's going to be all right."

"What happened, Doc," I asked with tears pouring down my face.

"Well, last night after you guys crashed, I went ashore with a flashlight just to confirm what I was afraid we already knew. I crawled under the shed in back of Sawyer's and spotted Yellow right away. At first I thought he was dead, but when I got next to him, I detected some labored breathing. He's a load, but I dragged him to the street and had the good luck to find a night-duty cabby. Even more fortunately, he knew that the local vet lived just above his office. So off we went, with Yellow holding on by a thread. Dr. Lopez and I worked on Yellow for hours, pumped his stomach and concluded that Bruno had fed him a hotdog stuffed with sleeping pills. Had he used strychnine or another lethal poison, we wouldn't have been able to save him, but some stimulants to keep his heart going did the trick," said Doc with a burp, (it was time for some Arm & Hammer).

"You didn't use obble gobble juice the way you did for Ole Tiger, did you, Doc?" I said as I gave him a bear hug.

Doc said that Yellow would need some special attention for a few days, then we thanked Dr. Lopez a million times and took a cab to the dock. When the three of us arrived back on the Sirius, Annie and Joey almost jumped overboard. Lizzie knew the story, but the kids didn't have a clue. From then on, no Mexican street dog ever got so much attention as Ole Yellow. He wasn't just a happy dog: he was a clean dog for maybe the first time in his life. When he was in Lopez's office, Doc had checked him over then given him shots and a bath.

By early afternoon we were allowed back on the Sumac. The Mexican police had cleaned it up. Not a trace of the messy business that had taken place the night before remained. The only evidence of a ruckus was a gash in the mahogany bulkhead where the spear had punctured Angel.

Even so it felt weird being back on the boat. I couldn't look at the starboard bunk, and I could tell that Joey was having trouble being near Doc's dinghy. It was clean as a whistle, but the fish bat that lay on the dinghy's floor was a grim reminder that the terror from the night before was not going to vanish just because the boat was clean.

My thoughts were interrupted when I heard people approaching the boat. The press were arriving and although they were supervised by Agent Paul, they took forever asking us questions, taking pictures and climbing around the boat. Doc complained bitterly, but Paul said it would do no good. From the Bryces' demise to the killers' deaths, the story was now international. Joey's and my pictures would be on the front page of newspapers all over the world.

Doc said we were celebrities. Even Yellow had his picture taken about one hundred times, which he seemed to really enjoy, but he was well overdue for a shore trip. Going from Mexican street dog to international celebrity was a big leap, but he still needed training on how to pee aboard a sailboat.

I hadn't been on land for a while, and my legs felt wobbly. I made it to the phone company office and placed a call to Maggie. It went right through and, unbelievably, she was there to answer.

"You'll be reading about me in the paper," I said.

"What have you done, gotten engaged to a beautiful senorita?" she questioned.

"Nope. Me and Joey killed a couple of drug-smuggling murderers," I said in a voice that I hoped would be believable.

"That's nice work, Andy. What else have you been doing to stay out of trouble?" asked Maggie.

"No, seriously. The ugly people on the dock in San Diego, they turned out to be the ones who murdered the Bryces, and yesterday they came after me. But Joey and me, we took 'em down," I said.

"Andy," she paused, "Are you OK. I mean, you and Joey, are you both OK?"

I gave Maggie some details, and before I finished, she interrupted, "I'm coming down. I'll let you know when. It won't be long – I've got to see you."

When I got off the phone, I looked at Ole Yellow. I swear he was smiling at me.

Chapter Twenty

Two days after the Sea Smasher left La Paz for San Diego, a high-level strategy meeting was held at the Washington F.B.I. headquarters.

Bureau Chief Jensen was boiling mad. His opening remarks dripped with sarcasm, "Now let me see if I got it straight. Senator Schwandel dies on Richard Ripardo's yacht near La Paz, Mexico. There is good reason to believe that he was in line to be the President's running mate the next time around. Am I right so far?"

"Yes, sir," replied the case supervisor, "But, there are more problems like –"

"Hold on, no more output. Just let me see if I've ingested the garbage pile you've just heaved onto the table," interrupted the chief.

The chief continued, "So we surmise that these two heavy-weights are doing more than just drinking gin in the sun. They're probably having some serious talks. Ripardo is known as Mr. Concrete in California business circles. With Schwandel's help, he could be awarded a federal contract to rebuild a freeway the length of the state. In return, Schwandel, who happens to chair the Committee to Re-elect the President, would pick up a pledge from Ripardo, a pledge big enough to make Ripardo the largest donor on the planet.

"So Ripardo figures it doesn't look good to have the senator die on his boat and he decides to pack him in ice and bring him back to San Diego, where a USAF cargo jet will whisk him back to Washington.

"Obviously, there is no way such a goofy plan could work – but wait, someone taps into the genius of our organization, and with expeditious speed, but absolutely no thought, we become partners in maybe the most asinine plot in bureau history. In fact, as we speak, a team of our people is ready to pick up the ice-packed corpse of the U.S. senator in San Diego.

"Ah, but the plot thickens even more. In one evening, two young boys have accomplished something that our Bureau of Narcotics team in Mexico has been attempting to do for months. They take down a murdering drug-smuggling couple that leave enough evidence to sink the world's largest drug cartel. Yesterday we nabbed an L.A. field boss and he pointed us toward the head schmuck. Where does that take us? Well, what do you know, we're back to the biggest donor to re-elect the President, the world's biggest cement mixer, and the world's nastiest drug king – none other than Richard Ripardo.

"I can see the headlines now, 'F.B.I. joins forces with drug king to smuggle dead senator out of Mexico.'"

Pausing to catch his breath, the chief continued, "Tell me, how many people in our organization know that we have a handle on Ripardo?"

"Only a few agents in the L.A. office, and they have been ordered to shut the lid," came a sheepish answer.

"Oh, wonderful. Then our worries are over. Is that what you're trying to tell me? Only three or four people in L.A., plus everyone in this room, knows that we are holding the world's hottest hot potato.

"You idiots!," screamed the chief. His face was

purple and the arteries in his neck seemed about to explode. "One consistency in the history of this organization is that never, ever, has a secret of any magnitude not become common knowledge.

"Gentlemen, the shit will hit the fan in less than twenty-four hours unless you pull off some sort of miracle. That yacht is making better than twenty-five knots. In about four hours she'll be out of Mexican waters. The bottom line is that the yacht must not make it to San Diego, Schwandel's body will vaporize, and Ripardo will fall into a very dark and very deep hole. Get on it!"

Chapter Twenty-One

The encounter with Angel and Bruno was so overwhelming that we all but forgot about the Sea Smasher. It wasn't every day that my little brother and I were in a battle to the death with a couple of murdering criminals, but sneaking Schwandel's body out of Mexico had the makings of another front-page story. The problem was that it was a secret, and the U.S. government agents intended to keep it that way.

The press had been mighty curious about where Mom and Mac were, but before any of us could say much, Agent Paul or one of the other guys would step in with the same pat answer, "Mrs. McCurdy needed some medical assistance and the owner of the Sea Smasher offered a quick trip to San Diego. Obviously if there had been an inkling of the danger that confronted her boys, she would never have gone. Mr. and Mrs. McCurdy will be arriving in San Diego tonight, and they will be back here tomorrow night."

I didn't realize just how much of a problem the timing of Joey's and my battle with Angel and Bruno was causing the U.S. agents. Because Deede Ripardo, just before departing for San Diego, had made a phone call to Schwandel's office, the feds were now involved in the caper. The plan to export Pumpkin Head was arranged under federal supervision, and secrecy was mandatory. So, the publicity about Bruno and Angel's demise was making the cover-up difficult. Agent Paul was offering little explanation for all the secrecy, but he did allow us one bit of information: orders were coming from the very top.

At least that gave us a partial explanation of why we could not reach the Sea Smasher by radio. Captain Blackburn had been ordered to maintain radio silence. Under no circumstances, except a mayday condition, were his radios to be used.

Doc had his Pacific charts out and was pointing out the Sea Smasher's probable course.

"They'll probably maintain a course four or five miles off shore, following the fifty-fathom curve going north. When they get to a threatening area, like this one near the Sacramento Reef, they'll head a safe distance out to sea."

"So when will they arrive in San Diego," I asked.

"My guess is they have the fuel to make it nonstop. With normal sea conditions, they'll be there by sunset tonight."

"That's good," I said. "We only have a few hours to wait."

Late in the afternoon Lizzie suggested we all go ashore for dinner, but she got voted down. We didn't want to miss a phone call, so we munched down some leftover spaghetti instead.

Around eight we were all getting antsy. Doc made up an excuse to take the dinghy ashore. When he got back, even though he didn't say so, I knew he had seen Agent Paul.

173

"Well, what did Paul say," I blurted out.

"Oh, ah, yes, I did run into him, but he didn't know anything. He said that they are a little late, but there is nothing to worry about. We'll hear from them in the morning."

I knew there were good reasons for not hearing from Mac and Mom. Maybe they had stopped in Turtle Bay for fuel. Maybe they ran into bad weather or mechanical difficulties. Even so, I didn't like not knowing. What made it worse was that I could tell that Doc was worried, too.

Sleep came in fits and starts, and when I woke before sunrise, Paul was sitting with Doc on the foredeck. I padded barefoot to join them, and asked, "What's the story?"

Paul and Doc must have agreed not to hide the facts from me because Doc started right off, saying, "The boat is missing and the mission has been canceled."

"What mission," I interrupted.

"Getting Schwandel's body out of Mexico," replied Doc.

"Our people in San Diego don't have a clue about the boat's whereabouts nor why the mission was canceled," added Paul.

The news struck me like a lightning bolt. All my insecurities of the past came rushing back. For a moment I felt like I had lapsed back into my first life.

Doc, sensing my despair, spurted out a string of reasons why we probably had not heard from them, like mechanical problems might have caused them to stop in some remote spot.

"Or maybe someone didn't want them to get there," I said, trying to hold back tears. "A big-shot wheeler-dealer like Ripardo probably had a bunch of enemies. The same goes for the senator. An airplane or fast boat could strike the Sea Smasher in open waters, and who would know?"

"We are living in a crazy world, Andy. Nothing is impossible." Paul paused. "There are a lot of lunatics that make rash decisions, but attacking an American yacht that's making an unplanned trip would require some sophisticated planning and timing."

"Not if the feds called for a covert air strike. It only takes minutes to get the mission going, and it's all top-secret. Mac knows all about that kind of stuff. He's told me how it works," I said.

"Maybe in a James Bond movie, Andy, but I don't see it under the existing circumstances," answered Paul.

After Paul left, Doc did not make my morning any easier by admitting that a Navy helicopter had made a search and found no sign of the Sea Smasher. I was in a major funk, but my mood had switched from feeling sorry for myself to hating that Potato Nose bastard. I knew that he was at the bottom of whatever had happened to Mom and Mac. If they had been hurt, I would dedicate the rest of my life to making him pay for whatever he had done.

Joey and Annie slept late. When they finally appeared on deck, Lizzie had a big breakfast ready for all of us. Doc made light of the news about the Sea Smasher but, even so, the kids were not fooled. Needless to say, a very glum mood prevailed for the rest of the morning.

Around noon I spotted Paul on the dock. He was running for his dinghy and, instead of rowing the short distance to the Sumac, he started his outboard. He began spewing out information as soon as we were within earshot.

"They're OK, they're safe!" he shouted. He jumped

into our cockpit and almost forgot to tie up his dinghy.

"Just got a call from the police in Ensenada. Your mom and dad are being driven to Tijuana – they'll be on an Areonaves flight this afternoon."

No one took their turn. Joey, Annie, Lizzie, Doc and I started a barrage of questions all at once.

"Stop. I don't know anything else. No, I don't know about the boat. I don't know what happened, except they are safe in a car somewhere between Ensenada and Tijuana. We will be having dinner with them tonight."

Chapter Twenty-Two

The rest of the day took forever. My parents had been gone for less than three days, but it seemed like years. I was only three days older, but I felt much older. Joey and I had each killed a person two days before. That didn't seem to bother Joey, but he had never lacked confidence from the day he was born. Annie was the same way. I guess Mom and Mac made tough kids. It wasn't that I was all shaken up and falling apart over the whole thing – I felt no remorse for what had happened to Angel and Bruno. I would have gladly given them the same dose of medicine all over again. It's just that I was a contemplator. I never had that huge supply of self-assurance that Joey and Annie were full of.

So I was looking forward to a one-on-one with Mac. Not for consolation because I really didn't need that. I wanted to hear his reaction to all that had happened. Being almost dead myself, and then thinking my parents could be dead was more than I could absorb. Talking it out with Mac would help me settle things in my own mind.

When Maggie stepped off the plane after my parents, my heart stopped. Seeing my parents alive and well was all that I had prepared myself for. The sight of Maggie arriving with them made my knees buckle. If Doc had not been there to steady me, I might have crashed to the pavement.

A massive family hug made Ole Yellow start to bark. Mac asked, "Who's he?"

"Say hello to Yellow, Mac. He's the latest addition to our family," I answered.

"Man, do we have some catching up to do," said Mac, with a smile.

I put my arms around Maggie and gave her a brotherly kiss rather than a passionate one.

"We've got a lot to talk about," I whispered in her ear. She nodded and gave me another hug.

As soon as we got back aboard the Sumac, I told Mac that it was time to take Ole Yellow ashore for a pee. (It wasn't really. Yellow could hold his water forever. Besides, he had already learned to lift a leg and let it go right between the lifelines. He just needed a little more training on selecting the downwind side.)

Mac took the cue and jumped into the dinghy with me.

"Hey, you guys," shouted Maggie. "Where are you going? Members of my family have been facing death, smuggling bodies and killing killers, and I haven't heard one detail! I've been waiting for two days and I'm getting sick and tired of it."

"Hold your water, Maggie. The sun's about to set and then it will be obble gobble time. Let's save all the details until then."

"Thanks a bunch, Mac," answered Maggie.

Lizzie jumped in with, "You shitheads better hurry back here." She was fired up already, and she hadn't even had her first belt.

"You go first, Andy, and start from the beginning," said Mac.

The First Life of Andy McCurdy

I began an unabridged edition of the last couple of days, including being molested by that hideous bitch.

Mac was relieved to hear that Doc had given me a "no sweat" pill and said, "When there is trouble, Doc is a guy you want to have around."

After a brief silence to let things sink in, Mac said, "You know, Andy, you and Joey found out some things about yourselves that some people never do. Men talk about how tough they are, but they really never know until they get an acid test. You guys have proven that you can face danger and react bravely."

"Maybe so, Mac," I responded, "but I remember how you used to say that the difference between a coward and a hero could be measured on the head of a pin."

"It all has to do with fear," said Mac. "Everyone experiences it, but the trick is to learn how to control it. I remember asking my squadron commander if he was ever scared before he flew a mission, and he replied that he hoped his crew chief hadn't seen his knees knocking every time he climbed into his fighter. That really helped me to control my fear. I figured if my squadron commander, who I thought was the bravest man in the world, was frightened, then fear had to be a normal reaction."

"Well, Mac, I was scared shitless, but I didn't fall apart. I prayed to God to give me courage. I don't know if that helped, or if it was the fact that I was mad because I thought they had killed Ole Yellow, and were terrorizing me, and might even kill Joey.

"If Joey hadn't rowed over when he did, I would have been off to the happy hunting grounds. His shout gave a split second of distraction, then everything came together. Angel took her eye off me for a moment, the spear gun loaded quickly, and Bruno leaned over the rail, giving Joey a shot at his head.

In seconds, it was over."

Mac put his arm around me and said, "All I can say is that you did good and I'm proud of you. You and Joey might still look like boys, but you have proven yourselves to be men." After a pause, he continued, "You were tested a little sooner in your lives than I would have preferred, but that's something that we really have no say in."

Talking with Mac helped me to get things in place. I told him that when I was being dragged behind the boat, all tangled up with the dead fisherman, I was sure I was going to die and, afterwards, I fell apart. Three nights ago, I thought for the second time that my life was over. I remembered thinking that dying before I reached my seventeenth birthday would be a real bummer, but I never lost control emotionally.

"Throw the dead senator into the mix and it's safe to say that you've had more hair-raising perils in the last two months than most people have in a lifetime," said Mac.

"You know, I was thinking the same thing last night. I realized that facing Bruno's knife was the end of my life. Now I am thinking that it was really the beginning of my second life – I just didn't have to die to get it started," I said.

"Do you mean that your life as a boy is over and your life as a man is beginning?" asked Mac.

After a pause, I answered, "No, not quite. I still want to be a boy for a while, but I think I've done some growing up. Maybe I've found the beginning of a foundation that might be solid enough to support some real values."

Mac had tears in his eyes and just repeated that he was super proud of me.

I thanked him for listening and said, "Now it's your turn, Mac. What happened?"

"Where to begin," said Mac. "Like I told Maggie,

we'll go over the details when we are all together, but some of the highlights are worth telling twice.

"We didn't have to fight any killers, but we certainly had a bizarre three days. Blackburn never left the pilothouse except to occasionally check fluid levels in the engine room. When we stood watch, he slept on the bunk behind the skipper's chair. The only time we talked at any length was when we were just off Turtle Bay. He took a hard look at our fuel situation then asked me to review his calculations.

"As for Potato Nose, Ripardo or whatever you want to call him, he took to his palatial cabin and only came out for the meals your mom prepared."

Mac went on to say that the trip was uneventful until they were intercepted by a Mexican gunboat just south of Ensenada. Then all hell broke loose.

"Before we get into the serious stuff, let me tell you about a little joke I pulled on your mom. She hated using the toilet because she had to look straight at the senator. She swore he was staring back at her from his icy tub. She knew he was dead, but looking at him made her sick. It was giving her a class-four case of constipation. So I put a temporary fix on the problem by covering poor Pumpkin's head with a bath towel."

Envisioning the senator, (who was rather gross even alive), now dead in a bathtub with a towel over his head, his body gently swaying to the roll of the boat, was a thought that struck my funny bone.

"Did it cure Mom's constipation," I asked between chuckles.

"I'm not sure," Mac went on saying, "but at about eight that night, your mom and I were in our cabin resting up before our turn to stand watch. Mom went into the head, and about one second later, she screamed, 'Mac, what are those beer bottles doing stuck in the ice with the senator?'

"That was a heck of a lot of ice for one dead senator, so I figured the old boy wouldn't mind if we got some extra use out of it," I answered as I grabbed a couple cool ones and began singing an old song we used to sing in Korea:

The night that Paddy Murphy died
I never shall forget.
The boys they got so stinking drunk
That some aren't sober yet.
The only thing they did that night
To fill my heart with fear,
Was when they took the ice right off the corpse
And put it in the beer!

"Good God, Mac! All these years and I never heard you sing that one before. What did Mom say?"

"Same as you. She claimed she'd never heard it before. But she drank the beer and felt a lot more relaxed about sharing a bathroom with old Pumpkin Head."

After another laugh, Mac continued with the highlights of their adventure. He said that the Sea Smasher was about twenty miles south of the Todos Santos Islands when they spotted a Mexican patrol boat heading in their direction. Captain Blackburn was napping on the pilot's bunk, right behind the helm. Ripardo, as usual, was in his cabin.

"'We may be having a visitor,' I said to your mom.

"With that, Blackburn leaped out of his bunk and grabbed his binoculars. Seconds later, he intercommed Ripardo to report that a Mexican gunboat was heading our way at flank speed, and that it would intercept our position within ten minutes.

"Ripardo entered the pilothouse, looking like

the wrath of God. He was drunk, blurry-eyed and unshaven. He looked more like a candidate for the dead senator's icy bathtub than a California big shot. He demanded to know what they were flashing. Blackburn told him that it was just one word – 'STOP.' Ripardo's response was, 'To hell with them – make a run for it.'

"But the captain said, 'No way. They've got at least a twenty-millimeter canon on deck and they're faster than us. We either stop or get blasted out of the water.'

"Blackburn tried to explain to Ripardo that the Mexicans most likely intended to board and we only had a few minutes to do something with the senator's body.

"But Ripardo was losing it, just like he did when Senator Schwandel croaked in the water. The sight of the gunboat bearing down on us seemed to drive him deeper into a drunken stupor. Instead of giving commands, he twitched, drooled, and occasionally farted.

"Blackburn took command, 'Come on, we have to dump the body.'

"Against my better judgment, Mom and I followed him back to our cabin. Blackburn spread a tarp on the floor next to the bathtub. Then, with all the strength we could muster, the three of us scooped the two-hundred-pound body out of the icy tub. Handling a gooey, giant jellyfish would have been preferable but, somehow, we managed to drop Pumpkin's body, face down, onto the tarp. He splashed like a bag of garbage, drenching us with freezing water.

"Then the real work began. We dragged the senator through the main cabin to the end of the stern cockpit, where a walk gate opened to the sea. Blackburn retrieved a large, rubber sea-bag used to store inflatable dinghies and the three of us slid the body inside. Then Blackburn scurried to the fish equipment locker and grabbed some lead balls.

"With a gigantic effort we managed to jettison the body overboard. We got some help, because just as we shoved the senator off, the boat gave a huge lurch forward. Both engines had fired into gear at full power. Blackburn disappeared like a shot and within seconds the boat was dead in the water again. The deceleration was so sharp that it sent both your mom and me flat on our kissers. We picked ourselves up and raced back to the pilothouse. Ripardo was on the floor. We guessed that Blackburn had knocked him down. The idiot had taken it upon himself to put the boat in gear and push the throttles open. Had Blackburn not moved quickly, the patrol boat would have opened fire and I wouldn't be here telling you this story.

"In moments the patrol boat was in close range of the Sea Smasher. A Mexican officer on the flying bridge shouted for us to put out fenders and grab their lines as he brought his boat alongside.

"An English-speaking officer accompanied by three uniformed men carrying AK-47s scrambled across the railing and onto the Sea Smasher's cockpit deck. Blackburn greeted them respectfully and ushered them back to the main cabin. Immediately two of the armed men started searching the boat as the leader began asking questions. It didn't take long before it was obvious they already knew a hell of a lot about us.

"'I assume you gentlemen know that it is against Mexican law to remove a body from Mexico without authorization,' was the officer's opening remark.

"He went on to say that his government took an even dimmer view of drug smuggling; a crime punishable by death. That got my attention, but then one of the soldiers returned, pushing Ripardo

The First Life of Andy McCurdy

ahead of him. The next scene I'll save for the gang tonight, but let it suffice to say that Ripardo's appearance was gross, but what came out of his mouth could have cost us our lives.

"He'd come out of his stupor and wasn't noticeably drooling anymore, but he was in some sort of an arrogant rage, shouting about how important he was and that his friends included the President. He screamed that no lowly beaners were permitted on his yacht and that they should haul their asses off right away or he would see to it that the wrath of the American government would crush them.

"When Ripardo finished, there was silence. I felt sure the Mexican officer was contemplating giving the command for his assistant to open fire. And I figured that if they shot Ripardo, they'd probably make a clean sweep of it and kill us, too.

"Fortunately, there was a distraction. I knew the officer was totally pissed and that wasting Ripardo was on his mind, but then a soldier returned to report that one of the heads had a tub half full of ice and that there was water all over the floor.

"The officer smiled and said, 'So that's why you are so damp. Dragging the dead body of an important man is hard work, right?'

"Even Ripardo didn't have an answer for that one. But we didn't have to stew in our juices long. Another soldier spotted a black object in the sea fifty yards off our stern. Blackburn was ordered to back up the Sea Smasher and, in minutes, we were reunited with poor, old Senator Pumpkin Head. Apparently his bloated body had more flotation power than two lead balls could offset.

"The 'body of an important man' remark was another clue that these guys knew a hell of a lot. I don't think Ripardo had figured that out, though. He launched into another unbelievably insulting tirade that could have gotten him shot.

"Instead of shooting him on the spot, the Mexican commander threw him an icy stare and gave the order to handcuff him. Then, he moved up close to Ripardo and calmly said, 'Señor, listen to me. You have no influence. Your friends are gone. Your associates, even your government, they do not know you anymore. You are a dead man. You can die now or later, it does not make the slightest difference to me.'

"Ripardo finally got the message. His arrogance melted away and he slipped back into an unintelligible slobbering.

"No time was wasted hoisting him, squealing and grunting, over the rail and onto the Mexican patrol boat. It took much more effort for the crew of Mexicans to transfer the sea-bag full of dead Pumpkin Head. The officer and one of his soldiers reboarded their boat, leaving the rest of us on the Sea Smasher. Blackburn was then ordered to follow them into Ensenada Harbor.

"That was the last we saw of Ripardo and the dead senator. Only a few days before, they were drinking gin, playing cards and counting the millions of dollars they had swindled. What a crashing downhill tumble they had taken."

"Holy cow, Mac, what do you think they did to Potato Nose," I asked.

"We have some theories, but we're not sure. Let's wait until tonight – Doc will be salivating," answered Mac.

"OK," I said. "But what happened in Ensenada and how did you get to the Tijuana airport?"

"The Mexicans were not after your mom and me. After being questioned at police headquarters, they checked us into a very nice motel. They brought in food and promised that in the morning we would be driven to the Tijuana airport to rendezvous with Maggie, who would be flown in from

Los Angeles. Reservations were all set for the three of us. Let's save the rest for tonight, Andy."

"Wait, Mac, who did all that? Who got the airline tickets, who contacted Maggie, and the big question – who called off the San Diego mission and tipped off the Mexicans?"

"Tonight, Andy, tonight," answered Mac firmly.

Rowing back to the Sumac, I asked Mac about the cover-up of Schwandel's death.

"I don't know," said Mac, "but it's undoubtedly part of the dirty politics in Washington – We sure picked a fine pair to go skin-diving with, didn't we, Andy?"

When we got back to the boat, Agent Paul was there. He had brought the latest addition of the San Diego *Union*.

"**LOCAL BOYS BATTLE KILLERS TO THE DEATH**" was the front-page headline. The whole story was there, even with a picture of Ole Yellow.

Paul said that we were on the front page all over the country and that magazines would want to cover the story as well.

"That does it," said Mac. "We're out of here at dawn tomorrow. A couple days on the beaches of Espiritu Santo will do this family a world of good."

"Good plan," said Paul. "We'll be watching you, so don't be surprised if you see a helicopter pass over every now and then."

"What's that all about," asked Mac quizzically.

"Drug gangs have a nasty habit of keeping score," replied Paul. "But in your case I don't think there's anything to worry about. Your actions were all in self-defense so there would be little reason to retaliate. Regardless, you guys will be kept under surveillance just to be safe. Espiritu Santo is a perfect spot. It's unapproachable by land, so all we have to do is watch the seaside. Odds are that nothing will happen, but if you see any suspicious boats coming your way, get on Channel 16 and start screaming."

Mac, Doc, Joey and I spent the rest of the daylight hours fitting a used prop that Sawyer's Marine had put together, while Mom, Maggie and Annie got supplies.

Just before sunset, Maggie suggested we go for a row. The colors of the clouds and the hills around La Paz Harbor were gorgeous as we paddled toward the inner end of the bay.

Maggie broke the silence by saying, "Did you get my letter?"

"I did, but I wasn't all that excited about it," I answered. "Too much 'you go your way and I'll go mine.' At least that was the way I felt about it a few days ago."

"So how do you feel now?" questioned Maggie.

After a long pause, I said, "I guess I feel lucky to be alive. That sort of supersedes everything else. While lying on that bunk waiting for that bitch to blow my brains out, a bunch of thoughts raced through my mind, mostly about things that I would never do, including having a seventeenth birthday party."

"Go on, Andy," Maggie encouraged.

"I guess I look at life with more appreciation now. It's like a second shot at things. Like I said, I'm just glad to be alive."

"And how does that all fit in with us?" asked Maggie.

I thought for a minute. "My feelings for you are as strong as ever, but like you said in your letter, we have a lot to learn about ourselves."

"That's true," said Maggie, "but during the past two months you've climbed some steep hills and learned a lot more than I have in my sheltered sorority life."

I started to say something, but as usual, when there was a chance to say something meaningful, nothing came out. I just saw the beauty of Maggie's face and thought about how much I loved her.

Then we slid to the floor of the dinghy in a warm embrace, reminiscent of our sunset evenings on our La Jolla beach.

"Let's take off our clothes," said Maggie.

This was not the first time that we had been naked together, but this time it did not end. Just the thin rubber floor of the dinghy separated us from the rippling water of the bay as we clung to each other so tightly that our bodies became one. Slowly, the gentle rocking of the dinghy brought on the effortless motion that consumed our minds and our bodies and took us together to the heights of euphoria.

When we awakened from our bliss, Maggie whispered, "The first time was ours, Andy. No matter what course our lives eventually take, the first time was ours."

"I agree. And that's a beautiful thought, but not completely accurate –"

But before I could finish, Maggie interrupted, "That didn't count, Andy. You were attacked. You were violated. Just the opposite of the love we just shared."

"Maggie, ten minutes ago was the most beautiful moment of my life. Three days ago, as my first life ended, I experienced the ugliest moment – but that moment is gone – gone forever. It died with my first life. Regardless of what happens, I will always remember what we shared tonight."

Then the darkness reminded us that it was

time to make our way back to the Sumac.

Instead of rowing their dinghy, Doc and Lizzie had powered the Sirius over and side-tied her to the Sumac for the night. I don't know if they did that to provide more security or for more conviviality. It didn't really matter, because our gang was all together again. That, alone, called for a celebration, and with all our new adventures to share, the gathering that night had major party written all over it.

Maggie and I tried to enter the cabin inconspicuously while Mac was offering a standing salute to Doc, "We made a big joke out of your danger signal, but it was your upside-down burgee idea that tipped off Joey. The fact is that your signal saved the lives of both our boys. Despite my skepticism, you stuck to your guns. We owe you a lot, Doc," said Mac with tears in his eyes.

Mom started to cry, but Lizzie cracked us up by saying, "Like I've always said, you sure are a smart son of a bitch, Doc."

And, as always, Doc retorted with a couple of his classic burps.

Being subdued was unnatural for us, but the mood lightened up soon. Lizzie had hopped over to the Sirius and returned with a (you guessed it) large, secretly-prepared bowl full of obble gobbles. I knew we kids weren't going to have any, but we were in for some fun regardless.

Maggie knew part of the Ensenada saga and I had a partial briefing from Mac, but Doc and Lizzie were totally in the dark and climbing the walls for some news.

"Well, would you like to start with a question-and-answer session," asked Mac.

"Hell no," retorted Doc. "Start from the beginning and leave out nothing."

The First Life of Andy McCurdy

So Mac began with the sighting of the Mexican patrol boat. When he got to the part about recovering Schwandel's body from the drink, Doc broke in with a question, "Why did the feds call off the San Diego plan."

"You're assuming the F.B.I. canceled the caper to smuggle Schwandel's body into San Diego and asked the Mexican police to intercept the Sea Smasher," said Mac.

"Who else?" answered Doc. "We know that the feds approved smuggling the senator's body out of Mexico, but why did they call it off?"

At that moment, Agent Paul, (who had gone off on some shore duties), rowed aside the Sumac and hailed for permission to come aboard.

After catching the drift of the conversation, Paul said, "Doc knows, maybe you all know, that I work for the Bureau of Narcotics in conjunction with the Mexican government. I'm not privy to all F.B.I. activities, but the notebook we found in Angel's hotel room led to the bust of her boss in L.A. He's dead, but he left tracks that might lead to the big boss. There is reason to suspect that person could be your yachting buddy, Richard Ripardo."

Mac broke a long silence with, "God all mighty, that makes sense. The F.B.I. wakes up to find they might have the world's biggest drug king as a partner in a simple plan to sneak a dead senator out of Mexico."

After a pause Mac continued. "So the F.B.I. concluded that they had a serious problem. It was bad enough to be part of a scheme to smuggle the senator, but what should they do when they came face to face with Ripardo on the docks of San Diego. They didn't have time to get the facts, and if they blew it Ripardo had enough influence to shut down the bureau."

Anxious to get the party started, Lizzie said

"This sounds like really serious stuff, but the ice is melting in the obble gobbles, and I hate mine diluted."

Paul responded, "Before a well-deserved celebration starts, I have a message that I have been instructed to share with you. You have all been involved in a matter that the bureau wishes to close. You already know a lot, and I have shared some highly-classified information with you. My job is to explain the importance of maintaining the absolute secrecy of all events pertinent to Senator Schwandel and Richard Ripardo. I know this is a lot to expect, but as trusted citizens you are being asked to erase the Sea Smasher incident from your memory. In other words, it never happened."

A moment of silence prevailed. Even Lizzie looked serious. Heads slowly nodded that Paul's message was clearly understood. Then Doc asked if some more questions were allowed. Paul said that was up to us, but he would only be a listener.

So Doc continued, "What did the Mexicans do with Ripardo?"

Paul shrugged his shoulders, but Mom spoke up. "On the way to the Tijuana airport our driver told us in broken English that Ripardo was a cooked goose and that he'd been taken to a Mexican prison. The driver did not know where, but he said that it would be far away. In Mexico some people go to prison and can't be found for months, sometimes years. Sometimes they disappear forever."

Except for the tinkling of ice in the obble gobbles, there was not a sound.

Then Mac added quietly, "We've all read stories about Mexican prisons that would curl your hair. Ripardo will probably be the center of some really ugly attention. Fat, repulsive gringos don't do well in Mexican prisons.

"Now that I think about it, I remember a message

The First Life of Andy McCurdy

the Mexican officer delivered to Ripardo. Just before they took him off his yacht, the officer told him that his influence was gone – neither his government nor his associates would ever want anything to do with him. He said that Ripardo was a dead man."

"Having his brains blown out by that officer might have been a welcome alternative for Ripardo," said Agent Paul. "But despite his sickening fate it's hard to feel any genuine sympathy for him."

Again we all nodded in agreement. I asked what had happened to the senator's body.

"We don't have a clue," said Mac. "He's probably rat food in some Mexican garbage dump by now."

"I doubt it," said Doc, "I don't know why, but getting his body out of Mexico was mighty important to some high-ranking people."

Silence and the sipping of obble gobbles followed. Again I thought of the sudden downfall of Pumpkin Head and Potato Nose. Doc revived the conversation by asking what had happened to the Sea Smasher and Captain Blackburn.

"Never saw Blackburn after Ensenada, but my guess is the Mexicans had very little interest in his detention," answered Mac.

"The Sea Smasher, now that's another issue," continued Mac. "I asked our driver if he thought the Sea Smasher would ever make it back to U.S. waters. He laughed and said that she was already a part of the Mexican Navy. They'd cut her flying bridge down to give her a lower profile, paint her green, red and white, and put her on patrol."

"Will our government let that happen?" asked Maggie.

"Why not? Ripardo is history. So anything connected to him vanishes, too," Mac replied.

The conversation shifted to how Maggie met up with Mom and Mac in Tijuana. Maggie said that shortly after my phone call, she was contacted by a woman who identified herself as an F.B.I. coordinator. She told Maggie how and when to meet Mom and Mac. Maggie already had her bag packed, so when she got the word she made tracks to San Diego.

Another round of obble gobbles definitely lightened the mood and Mac told a new rendition of me doing a pinwheel with the dead Mexican fisherman. Funny, but it didn't bother me anymore. In fact, I think I laughed harder than anyone else.

Then Lizzie took center stage with limericks. This thirty-minute, non-stop performance never failed to put us all into convulsions. She ended with an old favorite:

> *There once was a man from Alsace,*
> *Whose balls were made of glass.*
> *When they banged together,*
> *They played Stormy Weather,*
> *And lightning shot out of his ass.*

The funniest part of all was that Lizzie could never finish her rhymes without doubling up on the floor in laughter so contagious that soon we all had tears streaming down our cheeks.

"I'm out of here – good night, one and all. I'm pooped," said Maggie as she headed for her cabin.

The curtain came down shortly after that, and I volunteered to take the first watch.

Yellow was the only creature aboard interested in sharing watch with me, but soon he too fell asleep, and I found myself lost under a blanket of stars. After two months, the wonder of Baja nights still fascinated me. Automatically my eyes focused first on Arcturus, and for the millionth time I thought about light-years and how the light I was seeing had left that star thirty-seven years earlier. When my mom was just a baby, that twinkle had just begun its journey toward Earth. That really gets me, and I guess that's why Arcturus is my favorite star.

For the rest of my life, I would always have those thoughts. Mac says that when you think about yourself too much, it helps to think about the colossal magnitude of the universe. It helps put things in proper perspective. What may seem a gigantic problem at the time tends to shrink to insignificant proportions.

I had lived one life and had just begun another. I didn't even have to die.

I would not be bothered by God's shit list anymore. I know He doesn't have one. He's not sitting up there dressed in a robe, wearing a long beard, and keeping track of me. I don't have it all figured out, but I do believe that my job is to take care of myself. If I don't, I shouldn't expect God or anyone else to do it for me.

Of course, twice in the last month when the chips were down and I knew my number was up, I asked God for help. I still have some thinking to do on that one. I won't get it figured out tonight, but I won't set it aside indefinitely, either.

Mac's theory of infinity is perplexing, but I think I'll let him work on that while I concentrate on being a teenager. I think I'm ready to do that now. Before I almost died, my focus was pretty much all about me. I stayed within myself because I didn't have much confidence. That's all changed now. I'm ready to go back to the real world, and I'm ready to be a kid in high school.

As for Maggie and me, we are in love and always will be, but we won't inhibit each other's freedom. Only time will tell what becomes of us. I don't know who the love of my life will be, but if it isn't Maggie, she will always be my standard.

Most people go through life and never kill anybody. Joey and I are different, but one thing is for sure – we are not going to dwell on the negative parts of our experiences.

My nightmares of Angel and Bruno are over, so I probably should not bring this up, but I have a feeling that another chapter is yet to be revealed. Why I spook myself with this, I don't know, but sometimes I see a dark cloud on the horizon and wonder what it signifies.

That's just the way I am. I have finally learned that about myself. But I know that if problems come, I'll do my best to deal with them and I will never forget how lucky I am to have a second life.

THE END
OF
THE FIRST LIFE OF
ANDY McCURDY

EPILOGUE

Early the next morning, Agent Paul came to our boat with another edition of the San Diego *Union*. There was an interesting follow-up story about two brothers who had faced two killers, and a great picture of Ole Yellow, captioned "Mexican street dog finds new home."

On the same front page was an article titled: **"Senator Schwandel Reported Dead."**

> *Senator George Schwandel died today at his home in Washington, D.C. Apparently, he fell asleep in his bathtub and may have drowned. A family representative reports that the senator had been traveling a great deal and was exhausted.*
>
> *The senator was a key member of the Committee to Re-elect the President. His fundraising prowess, particularly on the West Coast, was significant.*
>
> *He is survived by his wife, Frances R. Schwandel, and his brother-in-law, Mr. Richard (Deede) Ripardo.*

Included was a long list of achievements and interests including his passion for fishing in Baja California.

Coincidently, a less conspicuous article appeared on the same page.

The title read, **"Dachshund Wins Best in Show."**

> *For the first time in the annals of the prestigious Westminster Dog Show, a dachshund has won the coveted honor of "Best in Show."*
>
> *"This is a true rags-to-riches story," stated the proud owners of the champion dachshund. "Less than a year ago, we adopted her through the Dachshund Rescue League. Apparently, she was nearly strangled to death by her previous owner on the courthouse steps of Oceanside, California. The name of our dachshund is Tricksy."*

I looked at Mac as we simultaneously said, "Oh my God."

CREDITS/THANKS

Credit and thanks for many years of informative reading about the incredible Sea of Cortez.

- John Steinbeck's *Log from the Sea of Cortez,* 1941.
- Richard and Silvia Gard's *Survey of Scammon's Lagoon,* 1970.
- Griffing Bancroft's *The Flight of The Least Petrel, 1932.*
- Leland R. Lewis and Peter E. Ebeling's *Baja Sea Guide,* 1971.
- Forty hand drawn charts perhaps by Ted Conant (can not find the actual name in my notes). 1964-1966.
- Editors and writers of *Sunset Magazine,* particularly Ray Cannon's *The Sea of Cortez.* 1966

Printed in the United States
62557LVS00002B/506